The Enchanted Snow Pony

For Annette & Nest, my fairy godmothers xx
—SARAH KILBRIDE

To Christine
—SOPHIE TILLEY

If you purchased this book without a cover, you should be aware that this book is stolen property. It was reported as "unsold and destroyed" to the publisher, and neither the author nor the publisher has received any payment for this "stripped book."

This book is a work of fiction. Any references to historical events, real people, or real places are used fictitiously. Other names, characters, places, and events are products of the author's imagination, and any resemblance to actual events or places or persons, living or dead, is entirely coincidental.

ALADDIN
An imprint of Simon & Schuster Children's Publishing Division
1230 Avenue of the Americas, New York, New York 10020
First Aladdin paperback edition November 2022
Text copyright © 2015 by Sarah KilBride
Cover illustration copyright © 2022 by Paula Franco
Interior illustrations based on artwork originated by Sophie Tilley copyright © 2015
Originally published in Great Britain in 2015 by Simon & Schuster UK Ltd.
Also available in an Aladdin hardcover edition.
All rights reserved, including the right of reproduction in whole or in part in any form.
ALADDIN and related logo are registered trademarks of Simon & Schuster, Inc.
For information about special discounts for bulk purchases, please contact
Simon & Schuster Special Sales at 1-866-506-1949 or business@simonandschuster.com.
The Simon & Schuster Speakers Bureau can bring authors to your live event. For more information or to book an event contact the Simon & Schuster Speakers Bureau at 1-866-248-3049 or visit our website at www.simonspeakers.com.
Cover designed by Tiara Iandiorio
The text of this book was set in Sabon LT Std.
Manufactured in the United States of America 0922 OFF
2 4 6 8 10 9 7 5 3 1
Library of Congress Control Number 2022936651
ISBN 9781534476370 (hc)
ISBN 9781534476363 (pbk)
ISBN 9781534476387 (ebook)

Princess EVIE

By Sarah KilBride

Interior illustrations by Sophie Tilley

The Enchanted Snow Pony

ALADDIN
NEW YORK   LONDON   TORONTO   SYDNEY   NEW DELHI

CHAPTER 1
Frozen Fountains

CHAPTER 2
Snowflake Surprises

CHAPTER 3
Fun in the Sun

CHAPTER 4
Moving Mountains

CHAPTER 5
Cave of Delights

CHAPTER 6
Snow Wonder

CHAPTER 1

Frozen Fountains

It was a chilly winter's morning at Starlight Castle. Princess Evie was cozy in her nest of duvets with the velvet curtains drawn around her four-poster bed.

As Evie snuggled up, she heard her kitten, Sparkles, push open the bedroom door.

"Good morning, Sparkles," said Evie, peeping out from the thick curtains.

"Meow," he replied cheerfully.

She hopped down from her bed and gave Sparkles his morning hug, then opened the curtains. Evie and Sparkles looked out of the tall windows and saw that Starlight Castle's grounds were white with snow and all the towers and turrets glittered with icicles.

"I think today's going to be a magical day, Sparkles," said Evie. "It's

the winter solstice, which means it's the shortest day of the year. Something special is bound to happen."

Evie and Sparkles didn't waste any time in getting ready. As soon as Evie had finished her breakfast of porridge and berries, they went skipping through the castle grounds to see Evie's magic ponies. They took the shortcut through the fern garden. It had been so cold in the night that even the fountains had frozen, leaving cascades of beautiful icicles.

"Wow, Sparkles!" said Evie. "They look like crystal crowns."

They didn't stop to admire the beautiful icicles for very long. They had to keep moving to stay warm. Besides, Evie could hear all her ponies neighing and getting excited at the thought of breakfast. She smiled from behind her woolly scarf. She loved every one of her ponies—they weren't any old ponies, they were magic ponies.

Whenever Evie rode them through the tunnel of trees, they would take her on the most amazing adventures in faraway lands. Everything changed when they came out of the tunnel— her ponies' coats, their bridles and saddles, manes and tails, and, best of all, Evie's outfits! Once, Evie had been a bridesmaid with a dress the color of bluebells. There she had met Bella and her mischievous pet dragon, Loki. They always made such lovely friends on their adventures—star princesses, ice pixies, and even mermaids.

Evie was brought back down to

earth as a sharp gust of wind blew from the north.

"Brrr, I'm glad I put my thermals on, Sparkles!" she said as she picked up her little kitten and tucked him into her coat. "It's no fun riding in the cold if you haven't wrapped up."

At this time of year, Evie always made sure she wore layers of clothes when she went out riding. She couldn't do without her woolly socks, scarf, and

thermal gloves. Even Sparkles appeared to be wearing an extra layer too—his winter coat was so thick!

"How about warming up with an adventure, Sparkles?" said Evie.

Although Sparkles was only a cat, he must have understood, as he started to purr loudly from under Evie's coat.

Evie unlatched the gate into Starlight Stables and took extra care as she made her way across the yard. There was ice everywhere and it was so slippery that she lost her footing a few times. Feeding in the wintertime always seemed to take longer, but luckily Evie didn't have to groom every pony. Her hardy ponies were happy to stay outside, as the oils in their coats helped to insulate them.

Willow, her New Forest pony,

Indigo, her Haflinger, and Silver, Evie's dappled Welsh mountain pony, all whinnied from the gate. Their breath misted like puffs of smoke.

"Come on, Silver," said Evie. "Let's go for an adventure."

Evie brought her pony in from the paddock and tied her next to a net full of tasty hay. Silver was one of Evie's smallest ponies—at only twelve hands high. But she was one of the strongest and most determined ponies Evie had ever met. Evie checked her pony over to make sure she was fit, and then

cleaned out her hooves with a hoof-pick. Silver sensed that they were going to ride through the tunnel of trees and began to whicker.

When Princess Evie finished this job, she walked carefully across the icy yard to the tack room, where she found Sparkles curled up on a comfortable old blanket that used to sit under Indigo's saddle.

"Come on." Evie smiled. "I'm going to tack Silver up. She can't wait to take us through the tunnel."

"Meow," replied Sparkles. He loved going on adventures with Evie and her magic ponies and never missed a chance to go through the tunnel of trees with them. They checked through Evie's backpack of useful things and added a few little extras—just in case.

"We've got one more job to do before we leave, Sparkles," said Evie.

She went to the feed room and filled a scoop with a selection of oats, cracked corn, and chopped apples.

"We mustn't forget the birds," said Evie as she sprinkled the contents of the scoop onto the top of the wall in the yard. "This weather can be really tough for our feathered friends."

While Evie had been looking after her ponies, all the wild birds had been searching for scraps to eat. Sparkles watched as Evie gave them fresh water in a shallow dish, and Evie noticed his tail swishing and his long whiskers twitching.

"Sparkles, I hope you're not feeling

hungry after your lovely big breakfast," she said.

Luckily it wasn't long before Silver was tacked up and the little kitten was perched in the saddle with Evie.

"I wonder who will be waiting for us," whispered Evie.

They rode away from the stables

and across the fields. Princess Evie
took a deep breath and closed her eyes,
as Silver tossed her thick mane and
trotted into the glittering tunnel of
trees.

CHAPTER 2

Snowflake Surprises

Princess Evie opened her eyes when she heard Silver's hooves crunching through a thick blanket of snow. She was surprised to see it was dark. Not as dark as night; more like dusk. There was no sign of the sun and the sky was heavy with snow clouds.

"I thought it was the morning, Sparkles," said Evie. Her little cat snuggled up to the lovely warm coat that Evie was now wearing. It was made of pale blue felt decorated with snowflakes and the collar was folded up high to protect Evie's face from the cold. Evie wore a pair of white leather gloves to keep her hands warm, and snug winter boots lined with wool.

Silver's mane and tail were decorated with glittering snow crystals and little icicles hung from her reins, tinkling as she shook her head. Evie loosened the reins and Silver lowered her head and neighed loudly, announcing their arrival.

The surrounding snow-filled valley seemed to absorb the sound. There was no echo and no answer. Evie searched the landscape.

"That's strange," said Evie. "Usually, there's somebody waiting for us when we come out of the tunnel."

The three of them looked around, but there was no one in sight. Suddenly, this stillness was filled with a shriek that made Sparkles, Silver, and Princess Evie jump. They looked up and saw a raven in the branches of a bare, black tree. He looked down at them keenly with shining eyes.

"Hello," said Evie, "were you expecting us?"

The raven swooped down and landed on the snow in front of them. He looked first at Evie and Sparkles, then at Silver, with his head cocked to one side. Evie thought that he might speak to them, but instead he cawed and began doing a funny little dance, hopping and zigzagging in the snow. He looked around at them with his bright eyes and cawed again.

"I think he wants us to follow him," whispered Evie. He flew up into the air, circled them three times, and then began to fly on ahead. Evie was right—he did want them to follow him.

Silver was sure-footed and sturdy, but had to take her time lifting her hooves high to walk through the deep snow. The raven waited for them on frozen branches, flying off again when Silver caught up with him. The promise of a snowstorm was growing as the snow clouds grew heavier in the sky. Evie hoped that wherever they were going, it wasn't going to be much farther. Then she realized that they were walking alongside a frozen lake.

"This looks like Lake Perla," Evie whispered to her pony, "where we went ice-skating with the snow fairies."

Silver whinnied and the raven crowed loudly from above and did a loop in the air.

"I think our raven friend is telling us that this *is* Lake Perla!" said Evie. "Oh, wouldn't it be lovely to see the snow fairies again?"

The three of them had had such fun with Sylvie and Trina, the snow fairies.

"What an adventure!" said Evie with a smile. "Do you remember how we rescued the little polar bear cub that was lost in a snowdrift? I'll never forget how brave you were, Silver. You pulled the snow fairies' sleigh through the blizzard, all the way to the North

Pole, and we delivered the polar bear cub back to his family."

Sparkles purred as he listened to Evie tell the story of their adventure, and Evie knew that talking to Silver was helping to keep her pony's spirits up.

"The polar bears were so grateful that they used their magic powers to help us fly back to the banks of Lake Perla where all the other snow fairies were waiting for us."

Just as Evie mentioned the words *snow fairies*, the snowstorm began and large snowflakes fell from the sky.

If only we could fly through the sky now, Evie thought.

She knew that plodding through thick snow was exhausting for her pony, and now Silver would have to plough on through the blizzard. It was so cold that when the freezing snowflakes landed on Evie's eyelashes they didn't melt. Sparkles tried to catch the flakes as they fell around him and Silver's coat glittered with those that had landed on her.

Evie looked up and saw two huge flakes swirling and dancing in the sky. As they swirled, they appeared to grow. They flew and flurried and

transformed into two shimmering snow fairies. They were Evie's friends Sylvie and Trina.

"Hello, Evie," said Sylvie as she fluttered down, landing gently on the fresh snow.

The moment Sylvie and Trina landed, the snowstorm stopped.

"Hello, Sparkles and Silver," said Trina, brushing the snow from Silver's coat. "Welcome back."

"I'm so glad you've come to see us," said Sylvie. "When we heard Odin's call we hoped that you had come through the tunnel of trees."

Odin, the raven, flew down and landed on Sylvie's shoulder. Sylvie stroked his glossy feathers.

"It's so lovely to see you again," said Trina. "And today is such a special day. It's the winter solstice and we are going to Queen Aurora's Midwinter Ball."

"Queen Aurora is the snow queen, the queen of the northern skies," explained Trina.

"Will you come along with us?"

asked Sylvie. "I know the queen would love to meet you all."

"We told her about our adventure with you and the polar bear cub," added Trina.

"Wow! A midwinter ball," said Evie.

"It's amazing," said Trina. "It's the best party of the year! We'll have so much fun!"

"Come on," said Sylvie. "We'll take you to a place where Silver can rest and we'll tell you all about it on the way."

"It's not far," added Trina.

The friends chatted as they traveled along the banks of Lake Perla with Odin flying high above.

"Every winter solstice, Queen Aurora has a party to celebrate the longest night of the year," said Sylvie. "You see, we live so far north that in

midwinter it's dark for most of the time. But from tomorrow the nights will start to get shorter and the days longer, and that is something we all celebrate."

"It's a big party with fairies and snow creatures coming from miles around," said Trina. "There will be a feast and lots of music, and Queen Aurora's Fjord ponies will perform their magical dance."

"And you can see the queen's famous display of northern lights in the sky," said Sylvie.

"It's the most amazing display you'll ever see," added Trina. "That's because the snow queen uses enchanted crystals found deep in the mountains. Their magic is so powerful that they fill the sky with dancing colors."

"I can't wait," Evie said, smiling.

It wasn't long before Evie spotted a little wooden shack on the banks of Lake Perla. It was painted white and was almost invisible in the snow, but its windows shone warm and welcoming. Princess Evie knew that

Silver was tired, but the moment that the hut came into view, she could feel her pony's pace quicken.

"Well done," she whispered, resting her hand on Silver's thick coat. "We're almost there."

"We'll take Silver into the hut," said Sylvie. "She can recover from all this snow walking in there."

"It's hard work, isn't it, girl?" said Trina. "But you're very strong."

Inside the shed there was some hay and water ready for Silver to enjoy. The fairies and Evie fussed over the little snow pony, making sure she was comfortable. Evie gave Silver a hug.

"You're safe and snug in here," she said.

"Soon the sun will rise and we will have a couple of hours of daylight," said Sylvie.

"And it will be time for some snow play!" said Trina.

CHAPTER 3

Fun in the Sun

The snow fairies were right—it wasn't long before the sky began to brighten. The sun rose and lit the snow-filled valley with a radiant pink glow.

"Now for some snow fun!" said Trina with a laugh.

"I'm still a bit wobbly on my ice skates," said Evie.

"Don't worry," replied Sylvie. "We're sledding today."

Sylvie and Trina picked up a pair of sleds that were leaning against the hut's wall.

"We've only got these two," said Trina. "You'll have to share with me, but that will just make our sled go even faster."

Silver pulled the sleds up the slope for them. The food and water had revived her and she was feeling rested. Sparkles loved jumping into the footprints that Evie left in the deep

snow. Odin and the snow fairies flew with their wings stretched out wide, warming them in the sunshine. By the time they all got to the top of the hill, the sky was clear and blue and everyone sat down to have a rest.

Evie could feel her cheeks glowing in the fresh air as she looked around the valley. It was breathtaking, with tall pine trees surrounding Lake Perla in snowy clusters and the majestic mountains sparkling in the sun.

"Sunlight is so precious at this time of year," said Sylvie.

"We always try to make the most of it," said Trina.

Sylvie passed around a pouch of dried berries. They tasted deliciously sweet and Evie felt a surge of energy the moment she popped them into her mouth.

"Shall we go down the slope first, Evie?" asked Trina. "You'll have to hold on tight!"

Evie sat behind Trina and before she

knew it, their sled was racing down toward Lake Perla. It felt as if they were flying and, although it had taken a long time to climb up, they were at the bottom of the hill in seconds. Trina and Evie landed together in a heap, looking up at the clear blue sky and giggling. They were covered in the

powdery snow and Evie was glad of her gloves and coat.

"We'd better get out of the way!" said Trina, as Sylvie got ready to whiz down.

The friends carried on playing in the winter sunshine until it was time to get ready for the party.

"Shall we get changed in the hut?" asked Evie.

"No," said Sylvie with a smile. "Here."

"But where are our outfits?" asked Evie.

"Here!" said Trina, laughing and spinning around in the snow. "All around us!"

"This is when the fun really starts," Sylvie said, taking Evie by the hand.

"We have to make our party dresses," said Trina.

Evie looked around, but couldn't see anything that they could use to make an outfit. All she could see was a mountainside of snow, some trees, and a frozen waterfall.

"All we have to do is draw what we'd like to wear in the snow," said Sylvie.

"Then we decorate our snow dresses with all the beautiful things around us," added Trina. "I'm going to use some of this reindeer moss that I've collected from the trees."

She opened her hand and showed Evie the pale green lichen.

The snow fairies and Evie set to work, helped of course by Odin,

Sparkles, and Silver. While Evie drew the outline of her dress, Silver scraped at the snow and found some velvet moss.

"Thank you, Silver," said Evie as she collected it with a little help from Odin. "This is just perfect for my snow dress's bodice."

Evie found some icicles on the

frozen waterfall in the mountainside and decided they would make a beautiful skirt decoration. Sparkles found some tiny frosty pine cones, and Evie collected a handful and laid them out on her snow dress.

"Look, Sparkles," she said. "Those cones make such a pretty belt."

Silver, Sparkles, Odin, and Evie all stood back to admire her dress as it lay

glittering in the snow. Sylvie and Trina had finished their party outfits too. Trina had used the pale green lichen to make a fluffy collar and cuffs for her dress of sparkling webs. Sylvie's dress shimmered with frozen leaves and bright berries.

"Now it's time for some snow magic!" said Trina.

She placed her hands on top of Sylvie's. The snow fairies closed their eyes and quietly sang

"Snow falling, frozen sun.
Ice mountains, blue sky fun.
Take the sparkling things we've found,
Icicles, webs, moss from the ground.
Then throw them up into the air,
And give us magical clothes to wear."

They threw their hands up and a flurry of snowflakes exploded from them into the sky. They were all the colors of the rainbow and they danced in the cold air for a few moments. Then they floated to the ground, covering all three snow dresses.

Princess Evie looked up and was stunned to see that the snow fairies were now wearing their beautiful snow dresses. She looked down, eager to see her own dress, but she was still wearing her felt coat.

"Oh dear," she said. "I don't think my dress has worked."

"Let's have a look," said Sylvie.

The fairies led Evie to the frozen waterfall and polished the ice until it shone like glass.

"Take off your coat, Evie," said Trina.

Evie undid the crystal buttons and took off her coat. She gasped when she saw her reflection in the frozen waterfall. She was wearing the party dress that she had made in the snow. The soft velvet bodice sparkled with frost, and the little belt made from Sparkles's pine cones hung prettily around her waist.

"Not bad!" said Sylvie, smiling.

"I love your icicle skirt," said Trina.

Evie twirled and as she did, her icicle skirt tinkled. The friends danced about, admiring one another's snow dresses in the waterfall mirror.

"I think we're ready to go to the party!" said Sylvie.

"I can't wait!" said Trina.

"Come on, Evie," said Sylvie.

But when Evie mounted Silver, she knew right away that something was wrong. Silver neighed and stamped her hoof in the snow. The little Welsh mountain pony's ears had pricked up and her nostrils were flared. She wasn't going anywhere.

"What is it, Silver?" asked Evie.

"I can hear something too," whispered Sylvie.

The friends stood as still as statues and listened carefully. At first, there wasn't a sound, but they all heard and then felt a low rumble that filled the snowy valley.

"Avalanche!" shouted Sylvie.

CHAPTER 4

Moving Mountains

Odin and the snow fairies flew quickly into the air with Sparkles in Trina's arms, but there was nothing Evie and Silver could do except hope that they weren't standing in the avalanche's path. Evie put her arms around Silver's neck.

"Stand fast, little pony," she whispered into Silver's ear. "We'll be all right."

Evie was trying to keep her pony still and calm, but she could feel her own heart racing as she watched the wall of snow come into view. The low rumble

grew to a roar and the sky above them seem to fill as snow crashed down the mountainside. Evie could see that the avalanche was taking everything in its path—trees and boulders—and she knew that it wouldn't be long before it got to where they stood. But as it came toward them it lost its momentum and grew smaller. By the time it got to the frozen waterfall, it had slowed down to a trickle.

"Phew," said Sylvie. "That was lucky."

Everything that had been in the avalanche's path had disappeared. It had either been buried or broken. Evie breathed a huge sigh of relief.

"Stay where you are, Evie," said Trina. "It takes a few minutes for the snow to set."

"After an avalanche, it takes about five minutes for the new snow to settle," explained Sylvie.

The valley fell silent after the noise of the avalanche. Then, out of the stillness came a voice crying, "Help! Please, somebody. Help!"

The friends looked at one another, amazed, and then the voice called out again.

"Help me!" called the voice. "I'm trapped."

"They sound as if they're deep in the mountain," said Evie.

"You're right," Sylvie agreed.

"We've got to get them out," said Trina.

"But how could someone get inside a mountain?" asked Evie.

"Good question," said Sylvie.

"Perhaps they fell down a ravine trying to escape the avalanche," suggested Trina.

"Or maybe they walked behind this waterfall before it froze over," said Evie.

"If we can find out how they got in, then we'll know how to get them out," said Trina.

"Let's take a look," said Sylvie. "But it'll be safer to fly as the snow might still be unsettled."

Sylvie, Trina, and Odin searched the mountainside for any crack or crevice that could let them in. Odin was quite

far when he cawed loudly—he had found something. The fairies fluttered up to the spot and Evie could hear them talking to someone. She couldn't wait to find out who it was and it wasn't long before the snow fairies fluttered down to tell her.

"It's Elva," said Sylvie. "One of Queen Aurora's snow maidens."

"She was collecting the magic crystals from the queen's mountain cave," said Trina, "but she's been trapped by a huge pile of avalanche snow. We can't get her out using that crevice, it's too small."

"We've got to find the entrance and unblock it," said Sylvie. "Without the crystals the northern lights can't happen."

"Elva told us that there's a large boulder at the mouth of the cave," said Trina, scanning the snow-covered mountainside, "with two silver birch trees growing beside it."

"Is that it over there?" Evie asked.

She pointed to a large, black boulder that was almost completely covered with snow. It lay halfway up the mountain. "I think you're right, Evie," said Sylvie.

"Come on," said Trina. "Let's take a look; the snow will have set by now."

Everyone rushed over to take a closer look and saw that beside the boulder were two little silver trees almost completely hidden by the

avalanche snow. They began to dig with their hands, but it was no good—the snow was too hard.

"It's going to be impossible for us to move all this snow," said Sylvie.

"It will take us days," agreed Trina.

"Let me see what I've got in here," said Princess Evie, opening her backpack of useful things.

As Evie pulled out a pencil and a pair of scissors, Sparkles found a long piece of string with a large magnifying glass tied to it. It landed heavily in the

snow and the sun shone down through the lens, making a bright spark of light to melt the snow beneath it.

"Well done, Sparkles!" said Evie, giving her kitten a hug. "You've found just the thing to soften the snow."

"We'll have to be quick," said Sylvie. "We don't have much time before the sun sets."

Sylvie was right—even though it had been light for only a couple of hours, the sun now hung low in the sky, ready to set. It was getting closer to the mountains by the minute, and very soon it was going to disappear behind them, leaving the northern skies in darkness again.

"We're going to dig you out, Elva!" Sylvie called through the snow.

"You'll be out in no time," said Trina.

The friends looked at one another. They would have to work as a team— and they would have to work fast.

Evie held the magnifying glass high up and aimed the sun's softening rays at the snow. Silver dug with her hooves and Sparkles pushed the melted snow

away with his paws. The snow fairies and Odin fluttered above, clearing the snow from the top of the entrance. They worked as hard as they could, their shadows getting longer and the sun getting lower. Evie could feel the air begin to chill.

"Look," said Trina, pointing.

They turned and watched the golden sun sink down behind the mountains, ready for the longest night of the year to begin.

"What are we going to do now?" asked Evie. "Even though we've moved lots of snow, we still haven't gotten into the mountainside."

The friends stood in the new darkness, catching their breath and looking at the huge pile of snow that they had moved. They were all exhausted.

"How are we ever going to get Elva out?" asked Evie.

"What will Queen Aurora say when she finds out that she hasn't got her magical crystals for her midwinter display?" added Sylvie.

"Perhaps we should have gone to her for help in the first place," said Trina with a sigh.

Silver walked up to the boulder. The little Welsh mountain pony dug her hooves into the snow and leaned against the boulder. Then she pushed with all her might.

"Look!" gasped Evie.

Everyone stared in disbelief as the little snow pony made the boulder move. It shifted just enough to make everyone realize what they had to do.

They all dug their feet into the snow, making sure they had a firm grip, and then pushed the boulder with Silver. Because they had melted and loosened a lot of snow, it wasn't long before they could feel the rock begin to dislodge.

"It's moving!" cheered Sylvie.

"We're almost there," Trina agreed.

The more they pushed, the easier it was, until suddenly they felt the rock tip.

"Stand clear!" shouted Sylvie.

They jumped back as the boulder rolled away from the mouth of the cave and down the mountainside, racing all the way through the trees to the banks of Lake Perla.

CHAPTER 5

Cave of Delights

A golden light shone from the cave entrance and Evie could see that there was a winding passageway that led deep into the mountain.

"Come on," said Sylvie. "Let's find Elva."

Odin flew in first, followed by everyone else. They went along the passageway that had been cut out of the rock and followed it around a corner. Princess Evie gasped in amazement; she had never seen anything so dazzling.

They were standing in a huge cave filled with golden light. The walls glittered with precious jewels and crystals of every size and color. From the ceiling hung sparkling gold and silver stalactites, like giant icicles.

Elva the snow maiden was standing in the middle of the cave with a basketful of crystals beside her. Her white hair shone and shimmered. It was so long, it almost touched the floor. The moment she saw her snow fairy friends she ran up to them and gave them a big hug. The snow fairies introduced her to Princess Evie, Sparkles, and Silver.

"Thank you all so much for coming to my rescue!" she said.

"We couldn't have done it without

Silver," said Sylvie. "She is the strongest pony in the north."

Elva was amazed when the fairies told her how the little Welsh mountain pony had managed to push the boulder from the cave entrance.

"But how could she?" Elva asked.

"Sparkles found a magnifying glass in Evie's backpack," replied Trina.

"And it melted some of the snow that had fallen in the avalanche," added Evie.

"That loosened the boulder," said Sylvie. "But it was Silver who thought of pushing it out of the way!"

"Queen Aurora will be so impressed," Elva said with a smile, stroking Silver's glittering mane. "We haven't got long before we have to leave for the Midwinter Ball, but as a reward for all your hard work I think you all deserve a little treat. Have a look around and bring me the stones that catch your eye."

Princess Evie looked around. The cave was encrusted with twinkling crystals of every shape and size. It was impossible for her to choose any favorites—they were all so beautiful. Sparkles, however, had found his favorite gemstone right away and was busy playing with a large, round tiger's-eye crystal.

Evie decided to choose stones in her favorite colors. She found a pink rose quartz and a purple amethyst, and then she spotted a glittering opal that seemed to have a rainbow inside.

She gave her stones to Elva, who closed her fingers around the jewels and gently blew into her hands. When the snow maiden opened her hands again, Evie saw a necklace of silver snowflakes. In the middle of each flake was a shining rose quartz or an amethyst, but there was no rainbow opal.

"I thought Silver might like that one," said Elva with a smile.

Evie looked at Silver and saw the

gleaming opal on her nose band.

"Silver, you look fantastic!" said Evie.

Elva made necklaces for the snow fairies and gave Sparkles a tiger's-eye pendant to hang from his collar.

"Now it's time for us to go," said Elva. "We need to get these magic crystals to Lake Perla."

Evie, Sylvie, and Trina helped the snow maiden with the basket that was filled with the crystals.

"These are heavy," said Evie. "Why don't we put them in one of the sleighs and Silver can pull it? You can ride with Sparkles and me if you want."

"Oh, thank you, Evie," said Elva. "I've always wanted to ride a Welsh mountain pony. The queen has a team of Fjord ponies. You'll meet them when we get to the palace."

Evie and Elva chatted about their ponies as everyone made their way out of the mountain. When they came out of the cave, it seemed even darker than before. The sky was clear and cold and flashing with stars. Evie noticed that the crystals were radiating their rainbow colors and everything around them was lit by their gentle glow.

Evie harnessed one of the sleighs to Silver while Elva loaded the basket of crystals onto it. Trina and Sparkles tied

the basket down so it wouldn't tip or fall on the journey to the snow palace.

"I've never seen jewels like this before," said Evie.

"They are magic and can only be found in this mountain," said Elva.

"Queen Aurora needs them for her display," added Sylvie.

"And she'll be wondering where we are if we don't set off now," Elva said, smiling. "Come on, Silver, let's take the

shortcut. All we need to do is follow Odin."

Odin was waiting for them by the silver birch trees. He turned and shot off down the mountainside toward Lake Perla.

"He knows the quickest routes," Sylvie said. "If we follow him, we'll be at the queen's palace in no time."

Evie, Elva, and Sparkles hopped up onto Silver and away she trotted, with Sylvie and Trina flying above. Off they all went, following Odin into the night.

CHAPTER 6

Snow Wonder

Silver pulled the sleigh steadily through the trees and down into the valley. Evie soon spotted other snow fairies making their way through the night sky to the party.

"Well done, Silver," said Elva. "We'll get there just in time."

Silver took them along the banks of Lake Perla to a flat plain. Standing around the moonlit clearing were lots of snow fairies in their glittering party outfits, fluffy birch mice, a snowy owl, some reindeer, Arctic foxes, and even the polar bear cub that Evie and Silver had rescued the last time they were here. He was standing with his family, but as soon as he saw his old friends he raced over with his mother.

"It's so good to see you again," he said.

"And you," said Evie, jumping down from Silver and giving the cub a hug. "You've grown so much since we last saw you."

"Thank you for bringing the

crystals," said his mom. "Without them we couldn't have the party!"

"This is the moment we've all been waiting for," said the cub.

Evie looked around, but couldn't see a snow palace or the snow queen with her Fjord ponies. The only things in the clearing were some strangely shaped snowdrifts.

"Will you help me, Evie?" asked Elva as she hopped down from Silver's saddle. "We need to put the crystals in the middle of the clearing."

Together, the girls carried the heavy basket into the center of the clearing and placed the crystals in the snow, their glowing colors reflected onto the snowdrifts, making them grow and change shape. Some of the drifts grew into tall snow towers and walls with icicle turrets, others into crystal tables laid with delicious feasts. Evie couldn't believe her eyes as she watched an amazing snow palace grow around them. Soon they were standing in a wonderful ballroom made of ice.

"Wow! You were right!" gasped Evie, astonished. "These crystals really are magic. What a beautiful palace."

Evie looked around at the glittering snow walls and shining crystal floor. The tall arched windows didn't have glass in them and looked out onto the snow mountains. Evie gazed up and saw that there wasn't a ceiling either, just the shimmering stars and moon shining down on everyone.

But most magical of all were the next transformations—the snowdrifts changing into Queen Aurora with her six magnificent Fjord ponies.

The caramel-colored ponies had dark stripes that ran from the tops of their heads and along their backs to their tails, making their flowing manes and tails a mixture of silver and black. Queen Aurora's hair was the same, and

it was so long that it trailed along the floor. She wore a sparkling white dress and a crown of crystal icicles.

"Welcome to the Midwinter Ball." The queen's clear voice rang out in the night air. "Let the party begin!"

Queen Aurora, Elva, and four other snow maidens mounted their Fjord ponies, who stood proudly in a circle around the crystals that were at the center of the ballroom.

"Silver and Evie," said Queen

Aurora. "Please come and join us."

Princess Evie was feeling a little confused as she led Silver to the center of the ballroom. How did the queen know her name? What was going to happen next and why did the queen want Evie and Silver to join in? She had no idea what to do. Elva directed her beautiful Fjord pony to stand next to Silver.

"Don't worry, Evie, Silver will know what to do," whispered Elva. "Trust her!"

Soft music blew into the palace on a gentle breeze. The ponies lifted their heads, whinnied, and then began to perform an intricate dance. Elva was right—Silver knew exactly what to do and joined in with the other ponies, dancing with them in perfect formation. They trotted neatly in diagonal patterns across the ballroom and performed slow canters to make the shape of a snowflake.

"I didn't know you were a dressage pony, Silver," said Evie as her pony performed a three-loop serpentine with Elva's Fjord pony.

Silver tossed her mane proudly while she picked up her hooves in perfect time to the music.

Princess Evie noticed Sparkles was in Trina's arms, watching the ponies perform their perfect dressage. He was spellbound, and so were the rest of the fairies and animals who stood at the edges of the room. Evie waved to him and he winked back at her.

The ponies spiraled around the crystals faster and faster. The crystals began to crackle and then their colors shot up into the starry sky. There was

an explosion of color that filled the sky with curves of light. The energy of the ponies' performance had completed the magic, and now the northern lights were beaming up into the sky from the crystals.

The audience went wild, clapping and cheering. The snow maiden riders, Evie, and Queen Aurora took a bow.

"What an amazing display," said Evie, looking up in wonder.

"You helped to make it happen," said Queen Aurora.

The queen's ponies all whinnied and whickered in agreement.

"In fact," added Elva, "if it hadn't been for you, Sparkles, and Silver, those crystals might still be in the mountain and the display would not have happened at all this year!"

"We're so glad we were able to help," said Evie. "We wouldn't have missed this for the world!"

"We have been looking forward to meeting you for such a long time," Queen Aurora said, smiling. "Trina and Sylvie have told us all about you and your brave snow pony Silver."

"Wasn't she brilliant in the dressage display?" said Elva.

"I didn't even know that Silver could do that," said Evie. "Or that Fjord ponies were so good at dressage."

"Our ponies are very sure-footed and extremely clever," said the queen with a smile. "Never underestimate what your pony is capable of doing. Now, I think it's time for us all to do some dancing and enjoy our midwinter feast."

The northern lights shone down, lighting the ballroom with flashing colors. The dance floor began to fill and soon everyone was having fun swirling and twirling to the beat of the snow fairy band.

Sylvie, Trina, Elva, and Evie danced together in their shimmering outfits while Silver, Odin, and Sparkles enjoyed watching the northern lights.

"All this dancing has made me hungry," Evie said to her snow fairy friends after some time on the dance floor.

"Me too," said Sylvie. "Let's see what there is to eat."

They went over to the tables that were laden with plates of delicious food.

"I don't know what to eat first," said Sylvie. "It all looks so good."

"It does, doesn't it?" agreed Trina. "I think that I'm going to try a little bit of everything!"

The friends tucked in and Evie's favorite was the Baked Alaska. The mountain of meringue looked as if it was made of sparkling snow and inside was delicious ice cream with crystal rose and violet flower petals.

"I think I might have to have another helping of that," said Evie. "And then it's probably time for us to go, isn't it, Sparkles? It must be getting late."

Queen Aurora came over as Evie was finishing her second helping of Baked Alaska.

"Thank you for coming," said Aurora. "It has been charming to meet you all."

"Promise us you'll come back," said Sylvie, giving Silver a kiss on the nose.

"Oh yes!" said Trina. "Come back

for our midsummer party! Now, that's quite a spectacular party too!"

"We'd love to," said Evie. "We've had so much fun. You were right, Trina. This has been the most amazing party ever!"

Evie mounted Silver, and Sparkles jumped up too, but when Evie asked

Silver to go, she wouldn't move.

"I think Silver wants to say her goodbyes too," said Elva.

"Of course," said Evie. "I'm sorry, Silver. We can't go without saying goodbye to your Fjord friends."

They walked over to the team of Fjord ponies, and Silver said her farewells to them by touching their noses with her own.

"Now it's time to go," said Princess Evie. "I'm beginning to feel quite tired!"

With a pretty neigh, Silver turned and trotted out of the snow castle. Evie was amazed how quickly they found the sparkling tunnel of trees. Before they disappeared into it, she turned Silver around so they could have one last look at the snow palace. The

northern lights shone down from the sky, filling it with colorful lights. Even though they were some distance from the castle, they could still hear music and laughter.

"I think that this midwinter party is going to go on all night!" said Evie, smiling. "But we need to get back and get some sleep. It's been quite an eventful day!"

Silver took them through the tunnel of trees and back to Starlight Stables, where there was still a sprinkling of snow that twinkled in the moonlight.

Princess Evie's ponies were glad to see them back safe and sound, and they whickered and neighed as Evie took off Silver's tack. Evie gave Silver some warm bran mash and checked her over. When she came back from hanging up Silver's saddle and bridle in the tack room, Sparkles trotted up to her, meowing loudly.

"What's the matter, Sparkles?" Evie asked.

The little kitten trotted across the icy stable yard with his tail in the air. He stopped and turned to meow at Evie again.

"All right," said Evie. "I'm coming!"

Evie followed her kitten across the yard and then saw what Sparkles was making all the fuss about. A sled was leaning against the stable wall. Evie took it into the moonlight to have a better look.

"It's beautiful," she said with a gasp.

The wooden sled was painted light blue and it was decorated with hundreds of snowflakes. Just like real

snowflakes, every one was unique! In the center of each flake was a tiny, sparkling crystal.

"Thank you, snow fairies," said Evie. "This is perfect. I can use it to help me on those icy mornings, and of course, we can have hours of snow play, can't we, Sparkles?"

"Meow," agreed Sparkles, chasing a snowflake that had floated down from the sky.

"It looks as if we might be able to use it tomorrow," said Evie. "I think the snow fairies have sent us some more snow."

Evie was right! As she and Sparkles walked up to Starlight Castle, there was a thick white blanket covering the castle grounds . . . and some very strangely shaped snowdrifts!

Pony Facts & Activities

Things Princess Evie Likes to Do on a Winter's Day

1. Make a bird cake for the hungry birds at Starlight Stables
2. Eat toasted crumpets
3. Make a hearty bucket of bran mash for all my ponies
4. Snuggle up with Sparkles in front of a warm winter's fire
5. Whiz about on my new sled

Silver

BREED:
Welsh mountain pony

FEATURES:
Hardy and very pretty with a small head and big eyes

HEIGHT:
12 hands

COLOR:
All colors except for piebald and skewbald

Northern Lights

Evie saw the northern lights with Queen Aurora, Elva, and the other snow maidens. This stunning phenomenon is also called aurora borealis, and it is a beautiful natural light display in the sky.

These sparkly lights are normally seen in the Arctic but can appear lower down in northern countries as well. Similar light displays happen in the Antarctic as well but there they are called the southern lights.

They come in all sorts of different shapes: swirls, curtains, columns, and beams. Some people even say that the northern lights make a noise—like the sound of lots of people applauding.

The northern lights were said to be named after Aurora, the Roman goddess of the dawn. People believed the lights looked like her cloak as she rode through the sky, opening the gates of heaven for Apollo, the sun god.

Other legends said that the lights were made when magical foxes made of fire danced and ran around, making sparks from their tails fly up into the sky.

Evie's Frozen Treats

Evie loved the special feast they had at the ice palace. Here's a recipe for you to make some frozen treats of your own with the help of an adult.

You will need:
An ice pop mold
Fruit juice of your choice, or yogurt
Fresh fruit, cut up

1. Pour your juice or yogurt into the mold, leaving some space at the top.
2. Add your chopped fruit.
3. Put the mold into the freezer.
4. Remove when frozen and enjoy!

Here Are Some Tasty Combinations to Try!

Summer Ice
Apple juice, strawberries, and raspberries

Totally Tropical
Mango juice, pineapples, and oranges

Strawberry smash
Strawberry yogurt and banana

Choconana
Plain yogurt, honey, cocoa powder, and banana
(mix the yogurt, honey, and cocoa together first)

Berry surprise
Grape juice and raspberries

Fjord Ponies

Queen Aurora and the other snow fairies rode Fjord ponies in the palace. Queen Aurora and her snow maidens used the ponies for a dressage display.

These beautiful horses are originally from Norway and are one of the oldest breeds of horses. There are records of them from the time of the Vikings.

They are very distinctive-looking! One of the things that makes them so recognizable is the dark stripe down their mane. In fact, their manes are often cut to stand straight up and show the dark stripe even more. Sometimes people say they have "zebra manes."

These ponies tend to be quite small but are very strong. Their coat is very thick so they can keep warm in the snowy weather.

True or False

1. Odin is a raven.
2. Evie brought crystals with her to the North Pole.
3. Sparkles is a New Forest pony.
4. The snow fairies make clothes from webs, moss, and icicles.
5. After the avalanche, Evie helped to rescue Elva, one of the snow maidens.
6. Evie met Queen Borealis.

(1.TRUE 2. FALSE 3. FALSE 4. TRUE 5. TRUE 6. FALSE)

READ & LEARN
with *simon kids*

Keep your child reading, learning, and having fun with Simon Kids!

A one-stop shop where you can **find downloadable resources, watch interactive author videos, browse books by reading level, and more!**

Visit us at
SimonandSchusterPublishing.com/ReadandLearn/

And follow us @SimonKids

 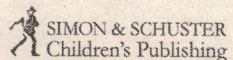 

SIMON & SCHUSTER
Children's Publishing

Looking for another great book?
Find it
IN THE MIDDLE.

Fun, fantastic books for kids
in the in-be**TWEEN** age.

IntheMiddleBooks.com

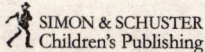   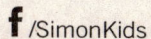   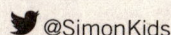

The Rainbow Foal

For Ygraine, with love
—SARAH KILBRIDE

To Flo, love from your Tatine, xx
—SOPHIE TILLEY

If you purchased this book without a cover, you should be aware that this book is stolen property. It was reported as "unsold and destroyed" to the publisher, and neither the author nor the publisher has received any payment for this "stripped book."

This book is a work of fiction. Any references to historical events, real people, or real places are used fictitiously. Other names, characters, places, and events are products of the author's imagination, and any resemblance to actual events or places or persons, living or dead, is entirely coincidental.

ALADDIN
An imprint of Simon & Schuster Children's Publishing Division
1230 Avenue of the Americas, New York, New York 10020
First Aladdin paperback edition March 2022
Text copyright © 2015 by Sarah KilBride
Cover illustration copyright © 2022 by Paula Franco
Interior illustrations based on artwork originated by Sophie Tilley copyright © 2015
Originally published in Great Britain in 2015 by Simon & Schuster UK Ltd.
Also available in an Aladdin hardcover edition.
All rights reserved, including the right of reproduction in whole or in part in any form.
ALADDIN and related logo are registered trademarks of Simon & Schuster, Inc.
For information about special discounts for bulk purchases, please contact
Simon & Schuster Special Sales at 1-866-506-1949 or business@simonandschuster.com.
The Simon & Schuster Speakers Bureau can bring authors to your live event. For more information or to book an event contact the Simon & Schuster Speakers Bureau at 1-866-248-3049 or visit our website at www.simonspeakers.com.
Cover designed by Tiara Iandiorio
The text of this book was set in Sabon LT Std.
Manufactured in the United States of America 0222 OFF
2 4 6 8 10 9 7 5 3 1
Library of Congress Control Number 2021948396
ISBN 9781534476349 (hc)
ISBN 9781534476332 (pbk)
ISBN 9781534476356 (ebook)

Princess EVIE

By Sarah KilBride

Interior illustrations by Sophie Tilley

The Rainbow Foal

ALADDIN
NEW YORK LONDON TORONTO SYDNEY NEW DELHI

CHAPTER 1
Sparkling Springtime

CHAPTER 2
Rainbow Reunion

CHAPTER 3
Scouring the Landscape

CHAPTER 4
Corolla's Special Day

CHAPTER 5
Petals Away!

CHAPTER 6
What's in a Name?

CHAPTER 7
Rainbow Wishes

CHAPTER 1

Sparkling Springtime

Princess Evie and her kitten, Sparkles, had been busy helping out with the spring-cleaning at Starlight Castle. The sun shone brightly through Princess Evie's gleaming bedroom windows and there wasn't a cobweb to be seen—quite an achievement, considering how high her room was! Evie opened her windows wide and the room filled with fresh spring air and birdsong. The sound of her ponies' neighs drifted in from Starlight Stables.

"Come on, Sparkles," said Evie. "I think it's time to do some spring-cleaning down at the stables."

Immediately, Sparkles stopped pouncing on a feather duster and was ready at the door. He always went to the stables with Evie, just in case they ended up riding through the tunnel of trees. You see, Evie's ponies weren't any old ponies. They were magic ponies, and whenever they went through the tunnel of trees, they took Evie and Sparkles on a magical adventure in a faraway land.

Together, they raced down the grand staircase. It was lined with portraits of Evie's ancestors sitting proudly on shining horses. Evie always stopped to look at one particular painting of

a young girl on a pretty pony.

"I'm sure I can see the tunnel of trees in the background, Sparkles," said Evie.

Sparkles rubbed his cheek against Evie's ankle, and then skipped down into the great hall and out to the gardens.

Although it was sunny, there was

a strong breeze that blew white clouds across the sky. Princess Evie and Sparkles decided to walk across the lawn and then take the short cut through the orchard. It was looking beautiful. Daffodils and crocuses danced cheerfully in the wind and green buds decorated the fruit tree branches. Evie and Sparkles even spotted a honeybee that had come out into the spring sunshine to enjoy the flowers.

"Don't worry, busy bee," smiled Evie. "It won't be long before these trees are covered in blossom, and then you'll have plenty of food!"

All the ponies at Starlight Stables neighed when they heard Evie's voice and saw she was on her way. They were always pleased to see her because Princess Evie was an important part of their family. Each pony loved Evie and had shared amazing adventures with her. Shimmer kicked her stable door as Evie walked into the yard.

"All right, my beauty," said Evie as she closed the gate.

She went to Shimmer's stable and smoothed her thick mane. Last winter,

Shimmer had taken Evie through the tunnel of trees to an ice cave where they had met an ice pixie called Freya. Evie always made the loveliest friends on her adventures, and that wasn't all—whenever they rode through the tunnel of trees, her ponies were magically transformed. Their coats became a completely different color and their tack sparkled with decorations. Evie's clothes changed too. When Star, her Arab pony, took Evie to the desert, she found herself wearing an outfit of purple silk and a pair of slippers that curled up at the toes.

Star was in the stable next to Shimmer's and, because it was such a fine day, Evie decided that Shimmer and Star should have some time in the

paddock. As soon as she turned them out, they rolled in the fresh grass and galloped around the field together.

"Right, Sparkles," said Evie. "Let's start with spring-cleaning our bridles."

Evie and Sparkles went into the tack room and collected some of her ponies' saddles and leather bridles. She carried them back into the sunshine and took them apart, making sure all the buckles were in good working order and the leather wasn't damaged in any way. She always cleaned her tack and made sure it was safe to use, but today Evie was going to oil it.

When tack became hard and dry, it was time to condition the leather with special oil. Evie got a clean cloth and poured a small amount of oil on it. She rubbed oil into all the different parts of the bridles—the cheekpieces, the browbands, and the nose bands. Some of them were quite fiddly! It was a slow job but a very important one. If the leather wasn't supple, it might snap, and that could be dangerous for Princess Evie and her ponies.

While she worked on Star's and Shimmer's saddles, Evie watched the ponies playing in the spring sunshine. She wouldn't be able to ride either of them for the next few days, because she had to wait for the oil to be completely absorbed before using their saddles again. Shimmer and Star were good friends, and Evie could see how much fun they were having out in the warm sunshine together.

Sparkles was in the paddock having a chat with one of his favorite ponies, Indigo. She was a beautiful golden Haflinger pony with a white mane and tail. Although she was quite small, Indigo was strong. Sparkles was especially fond of her because she was gentle and, while she had lots of energy, she was never impulsive.

Indigo and Sparkles trotted over to watch as Evie finished cleaning the

tack and put everything back together.

"Would you two like to go through the tunnel of trees today?" asked Princess Evie.

Even though Sparkles was only a cat, Evie knew he could understand every word she said. As soon as he heard Evie mention the tunnel of trees, Sparkles meowed and jumped onto the gate and into the yard. He followed Evie into the tack room, where she hung up the bridles and saddles, then got Indigo's halter and the grooming kit. Before she could saddle her pony, she would have to brush out Indigo's coat.

It always took a little longer at this time of year. All of Evie's hardy ponies—Silver the Welsh mountain, Willow the New Forest, and, of course,

Indigo, had spent the winter out in the fields. At the beginning of spring, they still had thick winter coats. Evie loved brushing this hair out to gradually reveal her ponies' beautiful summer coats. Their colors and markings became lighter and more defined; even the swirls and whorls seemed shinier. And it wasn't just Evie who loved the process of brushing out the ponies' winter coats. A row of sparrows and blue nuthatches was already waiting on the stable roof for the soft hair that made a warm lining for their nests.

"Let's do some spring-cleaning with you, Indigo," said Evie, tying her pony up.

Evie started by cleaning out her Haflinger's hooves. Then she brushed Indigo's golden coat with the dandy brush. When Evie had finished grooming, there were clumps of hair blowing around the stable yard. The twittering birds that had been watching flew down from the roof and began to collect the hair.

As Evie tacked her pony up, the clouds darkened. Her other ponies went to stand under the trees and in the field shelters.

"It looks as if there's going to be a spring shower, Sparkles," said Evie. "Come on, let's get our backpack of useful things. If we're quick, we should miss the rain."

Sparkles found Evie's backpack hanging by Shimmer's hay net. They could never go through the tunnel of trees without it—there was always something in there that they needed on their adventure. Evie put on her backpack and mounted Indigo. Sparkles jumped up after her. They were ready for an adventure. Evie loved riding Indigo. Haflinger ponies are quite light on their feet, and Indigo had a lovely balanced action. As soon as they were out of the stable yard, the first drops of spring rain began to fall.

Indigo broke into a smooth canter and made her way across the fields, toward the tunnel of trees. "I wonder where the tunnel will take us today," said Evie.

CHAPTER 2

Rainbow Reunion

As soon as they came out of the tunnel of trees, they saw a host of butterflies fluttering around them. Ahead of them was a shimmering rainbow, and Evie knew exactly where it would lead them.

"Hooray!" said Evie. "We're heading to the Rainbow Garden. I hope we're going to see Violet and all the other Rainbow Girls again."

Indigo whinnied and shook her long mane, which was now beautiful shades of pink. Her coat swirled and shone

and seemed to reflect all the colors of the rainbow. Evie's flowing dress was patterned like the butterflies' wings, with pretty sleeves that quivered in the breeze.

"Come on, Indigo," said Evie happily. "I'm sure you can remember the way!"

Without any hesitation, Indigo started to climb up the rainbow, following the delicate butterflies into the clouds. Soon she trotted out into the Rainbow Garden, where, sure enough, Evie's old friend Violet was waiting for them.

"Oh, Indigo, you clever pony!" said Violet, stroking the pretty pony's nose. "I knew you'd come back to see us. Well done for remembering the way!"

"Violet," smiled Evie, "it's so lovely to see you again."

Evie hopped down and gave her friend a hug.

"And you, Evie," said Violet. "I can't wait to tell the other Rainbow Girls that you're here."

Violet led them through the Rainbow Garden. The garden was blooming with

exotic flowers of every shape and size.
There were fragile orchids growing
in the trees, tall red lilies that looked
like flaming trumpets, and pretty pink
mimosas with leaves that snapped shut
when you touched them. The air was
filled with the fragrance of tiny jasmine
flowers. As they walked through the

wonderful garden, the friends recalled their last adventure together.

"Do you remember the first time you saw this garden?" said Violet. "There were no colors in it at all!"

"How could I forget?" Evie replied. "I was so disappointed. Everything was gray— the flowers, the trees, even the lawns!"

Evie, Sparkles, and Indigo had helped

to return color to the Rainbow Garden by collecting precious gemstones from each of the Rainbow Girls. When Evie put the gemstones into the magic well, the garden filled with rainbow bubbles and all the flowers returned to their beautiful shades.

"If you, Sparkles, and your magic rainbow pony hadn't come to visit us, this garden would still be gray," said Violet. "You are a great team."

Toward the end of the garden they found Rosa's gazebo, where all the Rainbow Girls were working hard. They were so busy that at first, no one noticed Evie and Violet arrive. Azure and Fern were cutting tiny petals from a huge piece of white silk. Magenta and Rosa were painting the edges of

the heart-shaped petals with the palest of pinks, yellows, and greens. Evie could see Saffron and Amber in the gazebo making some food. It smelled delicious!

It was Rosa who saw Evie first. She put down her paintbrush and ran over to give Evie a hug. It wasn't long before all the Rainbow Girls surrounded Evie, Sparkles, and Indigo.

Rosa, Magenta, Saffron, Amber, Fern, and Azure were all chatting away at once and welcoming them with smiles and kisses.

"It's so exciting that you've returned," said Rosa.

"How fantastic that you've come today, Evie," said Magenta as she gave Sparkles a hug. "It's one of the busiest days of the year."

"Today is the start of our Rainbow Blossom Festival, and we've got lots of jobs to do before the festival can begin," added Rosa.

"Come on, Evie," said Amber, taking Evie by the hand. "Let's sit down and we'll tell you all about it."

There was a cluster of rainbow-colored cushions underneath the apple tree.

Everyone got comfy, especially Sparkles, who sat on Evie's knee and listened carefully to the Rainbow Girls.

"Every year, visitors come from far and wide to enjoy the beautiful blossoms in our Rainbow Garden," said Violet.

"But first we have to make the blossoms from this very special silk," said Rosa. She held up the material and the sun shone through it, making it shimmer.

"Azure and I have to cut each petal perfectly," said Fern. "It takes a lot of concentration."

"Then Magenta and I paint them," said Rosa.

"Just around the edges, so each petal has a hint of color," added Magenta.

"My job is to prepare our pony, Corolla, and our chariot," smiled Violet. "She will take us through the air when it's time to sprinkle the trees with our beautiful blossoms."

"Then we can relax under the trees and eat our delicious picnic and sing flower songs," added Fern. "Just like everyone else!"

"It's Fern's and my job to prepare the feast," continued Azure.

"So you see," said Violet, "we could

do with an extra pair of hands and paws, and maybe even another set of hooves!"

"We'd be happy to help you," said Evie, "wouldn't we?"

Sparkles purred and Indigo neighed.

"Thank you, Evie," said Rosa. "We can always count on you."

"Will you come with me to the yard and prepare the chariot please?" Violet asked Evie. "It needs a good spring clean, and we'll have to give Corolla an extra groom as this is her special day."

"We'll have her ready in no time!" said Evie.

"Brilliant!" smiled Magenta. "We'll meet you down at the yard at midday."

CHAPTER 3

Scouring the Landscape

Evie and Sparkles mounted Indigo.
"Come on up, Violet," she said.
"There's room for the three of us."
Indigo trotted away, taking Evie, Violet, and Sparkles to the yard. It wasn't far, and when they got there Evie tied Indigo up and gave her some fresh water and hay. Violet opened the shed door and took her friend inside. Evie gasped when she saw the chariot. Even though the shed was gloomy, she could see that the carriage was

decorated with rainbow jewels and had wheels of silver.

"We only use this chariot for the Rainbow Blossom Festival," said Violet. "It needs a really good clean."

Together, Violet and Evie pulled the chariot out into the sunlight. Even though it was quite dusty, it was beautiful.

The friends sorted through cloths, brushes, and sponges, and filled a bucket with soapy water. Sparkles had a lot of fun chasing the frothy

bubbles while Violet and Evie swept and scrubbed and polished. They weren't just cleaning the chariot to make it look spectacular. They were cleaning it for the same reasons that Evie had to clean her tack, to make sure that it was in good condition and was safe to use. While the girls worked, they checked all the nuts and bolts and oiled each moving part, making certain that everything was in good, working order.

"I cleaned the harness earlier this morning, but I think I may have to adjust some of the straps as Corolla has grown rounder this spring!" said Violet.

Evie laughed. "Yes, some of my ponies get carried away at this time of year. I think it's all the fresh grass."

As Violet undid some of the silver

buckles and loosened the straps, Evie looked at the gleaming harness closely.

"This doesn't look like any of the driving harnesses I've seen before," she said.

"That's because there's something a bit different about Corolla," said Violet with a smile. "She's got wings and can fly through the air!"

"Like Pegasus!" said Evie. "I've read the myth in Starlight Castle's library, but I never thought I'd ever meet a winged horse."

"Well, today is your lucky day," said Violet. "She's a real beauty. You'll see when we get her in from the fields. And this year she's in such good condition, she's radiant. She's had a sparkle in her eyes for the past few weeks. I think she's been looking forward to today."

"I can't wait to meet her," said Evie. "I don't think Indigo can either."

Sure enough, Indigo sniffed the air and whinnied loudly, but there was no reply.

"She's probably too busy eating!" said Violet, polishing the silver wheel

spokes. "She knows that it's her special day, and she'll need lots of energy. We'll bring her in when we've finished here."

Evie brushed the dust off the gemstones and then washed them gently with a damp cloth. Finally, she polished each jewel with a duster until every facet shone magnificently.

Soon the girls stood back to admire

their work. The chariot glittered in the spring sunshine.

"Amazing!" said Evie.

"You wait," said Violet. "It looks even more wonderful when Corolla is pulling it through the sky!"

Violet collected Corolla's halter and they made their way to the paddock. But when they arrived, there was no pony.

"That's strange," said Violet. "She normally waits by the gate when she hears me coming."

Evie scanned the field but could see no sign of the pony. Violet called her name and Indigo whinnied, but Corolla didn't appear. Evie could see that her friend was worried.

"Let's go in and have a good look," said Evie. "She can't have gone far.

Perhaps she's in her shelter or behind those trees."

Sparkles hopped through the gate, his whiskers twitching. Violet opened the gate and Evie followed her into the field. They walked to the shelter, calling Corolla's name. They looked behind the trees, but there was no winged pony.

"Could she have flown off to another field?" asked Evie.

"She has never done that before," said Violet. "Although, this morning she was very unsettled. She kept lying down, then getting up and walking around as if she was uncomfortable."

"Perhaps she was feeling nervous," suggested Evie.

"Perhaps," said Violet. "I'll get some food to rattle in a bucket. Hopefully, she'll hear it and fly back here."

"Good idea," said Evie, smiling. "That usually works!"

While Evie waited for her friend, she called the pony's name again. Violet returned with the bucket of food and shook it loudly.

They waited for a few minutes,

hoping to hear the sound of Corolla's wings or perhaps a neigh, but there was nothing.

"We'll find her, Violet," said Evie quietly.

"I hope she's all right," said Violet.

The girls looked around the paddock, even though it was obvious that Corolla was not there.

"I'm sure she's okay," said Evie reassuringly, holding Violet's hand. "Ponies sometimes do strange things when they know something special is about to happen. She can't have gone far."

Violet tried to smile.

"Should we let the other girls know?" asked Evie.

"Let's go to the top of the field," said Violet. "We'll get a good view of the Rainbow Valley from there. If we can't see her, then we'll have to send out search parties."

The girls, Indigo, and Sparkles raced to the top of the field. Violet was right. They could see for miles and it was breathtaking. Rainbows arched over the rolling green hills and small rain clouds hovered over parts of the valley. While the girls searched for Corolla, Sparkles played with the string of Evie's backpack as if he was trying to untie it.

"Of course, Sparkles!" said Evie. "There must be something in here

that will help us." She opened up her backpack of useful things and the very first thing that she pulled out was an old brass telescope.

"Perfect!" said Evie. "Now we can see even farther."

She held the telescope up to her eye. Where could Corolla be?

CHAPTER 4

Corolla's Special Day

Evie passed the telescope to Violet.

"Do you want to have a look? After all, you know what your pony looks like."

Violet took the telescope and moved it slowly along the horizon. Suddenly, she stopped and turned the lens slightly to focus.

"There she is!" she cried.

Evie and Violet cheered and Sparkles purred, while Indigo let out a happy whinny. Evie could see how relieved Violet was. "She's at the edge of Kaleidoscope Wood!"

"Is she all right?" asked Evie.

"I can't see. She's too far away."

"Indigo, we need you to take us to Corolla as fast as you can!" said Evie. She jumped up into the saddle, followed by Violet and Sparkles.

"I'll tell you the way," said Violet as Indigo broke into a gallop over the field.

Soon they were racing toward a gate. Indigo seemed to sense there was no

time for the girls to dismount and open it, so she leaped over the gate.

"That's it, Indigo," called Evie as the wind whistled past them. "We're almost there."

They raced along the slopes and were soon in the field that lay next to Kaleidoscope Wood. There, standing by the trees, was a dappled pony. As they got closer, Evie noticed her coat was similar to a blue roan pony's, except, instead of it being a blue-gray color, it was violet. Her wings were folded tightly against her body but Evie could see they sparkled with delicate markings, like a butterfly's wings. The most striking thing about this pony was how much she was sweating. Her mane was wet and her coat was dripping.

"Corolla," said Violet softly, getting down from Indigo.

Corolla took a step back. She was breathing fast and looked agitated. Her eyes were full of fear and she was letting out short, sharp neighs. . . .

"We need to get help," said Violet. "I've never seen her like this before."

"I'll go," said Evie. "You stay with your pony, she needs you. Shall I go to Rosa's gazebo?"

"No," said Violet. "This is serious. We need the vet, Ginny Martingale; she'll know what's wrong."

"Where will she be?" asked Evie.

"Just follow the stream to the bottom of the valley. Her cottage will be the first one you come to; it's next to the bridge."

"Be brave, Violet," said Evie, giving her friend a hug. "We'll bring Ginny back as quickly as we can and she'll help Corolla get better. Try not to worry, Corolla is a strong pony."

As Evie made her way on Indigo, she thought about what could be wrong with Corolla. Perhaps she had colic— she was showing all the symptoms. Or worse still, maybe she had eaten something poisonous. Whatever it was, the poor pony was in pain and a lot of distress.

It only took a few minutes for Evie, Indigo, and Sparkles to arrive at the vet's cottage.

"Please, come quickly," said Evie

as Ginny opened her front door.

"Whatever is the matter?" asked the vet.

"The Rainbow Girls' pony, Corolla, is sick," said Evie, trying to catch her breath. "She's sweating, and I think she's in a lot of pain."

"Where is the poor thing?" asked Ginny as she grabbed her vet's bag.

"Violet is with her at the edge of the wood," Evie replied. "She's never seen Corolla like this before."

"Violet was right to send for me," said Ginny. "We need to get there quickly."

But they were too late. When Ginny and Princess Evie arrived at Kaleidoscope Wood, they found Violet standing by Corolla, looking pale and shaken. Corolla looked brighter than the last time Evie had seen her. Her eyes shone and she stood calmly, whickering quietly. There was something else—Evie could see an extra set of very long, spindly legs.

Corolla moved slightly and Evie saw the most beautiful rainbow-colored foal standing beside her. Its coat swirled and shimmered, and its fluffy mane and tail were the color of sunsets. Although it had only been born a few minutes ago, it was already standing unsteadily and shaking its small wings. It looked up at its mother with bright eyes, and when it blinked, Evie noticed how long and sparkly its eyelashes were.

"Are you all right, Violet?" asked Ginny.

"I think so," said Violet, not sounding very sure.

"Perhaps Evie could look after you for a minute," said Ginny. "While I check mom and foal. They both look well, but you can never be too sure."

Evie took Violet by the hand and led her to sit down on the soft grass.

"It all happened so quickly," said Violet. "One minute a pair of tiny hooves appeared, and the next, there was this beautiful foal."

"It's a miracle!" said Evie.

"It explains why Corolla has been looking so well," smiled Violet. "And why she put on all that weight!"

"And it explains why she was behaving so strangely this morning," added Evie. "Well, you did say that today was her special day."

Ginny came over and sat next to the girls.

"Corolla and her foal are fine," said the vet. "Well done, Violet. Your pony knew you were there for her in case something went wrong, and you helped her to give birth safely by standing back and not disturbing her. It's tough, and can be traumatic, but ponies instinctively know what to do."

Ginny had given Corolla and her foal a checkup, making certain that they were both healthy.

"The first twenty-four hours of the foal's life are the most important," she said. "They need to be able to stand in the first hour and feed in the second—that's when their bodies are able to absorb the most antibodies from their mother's milk."

They all watched as Corolla's foal began to suckle. Corolla was gently whickering and sniffing her baby's coat.

"It looks like Corolla is going to be a great first-time mom," smiled Ginny. "She's bonding with her baby and connecting with her through all the senses. Her foal's senses will develop

fully over the next couple of weeks."

"Do some ponies not bond with their foals?" asked Evie.

"You have to watch new moms carefully. Sometimes their maternal instinct isn't very strong, or they may still be suffering after giving birth," said the vet. "But it's important not to interfere with the first contact unless you have to. All these two need now is to be alone, to bond and recover."

The friends looked at each other, sharing the same thought.

"Corolla won't be able to draw the Rainbow Blossom Chariot this year, will she?" asked Violet.

"I'm sorry, but that's completely out of the question," smiled Ginny. "She needs time to rest."

"Of course, she's exhausted after delivering her foal," said Evie. "But what are we going to do for the Rainbow Blossom Festival?"

"I think I have an idea who could pull the Rainbow Blossom Chariot for us," said Violet, gazing at Indigo. "What do you think, Evie?"

Evie guessed what her friend was

thinking and smiled. Indigo stopped munching the grass and looked up at the girls. She blinked at them as if she knew what Evie was going to say next.

"Indigo," said Evie. "How would you like to pull the Rainbow Blossom Chariot this year?"

CHAPTER 5

Petals Away!

"Has Indigo ever drawn a carriage or a cart before?" asked Violet.

"We had a go once and she enjoyed it," said Evie. "Haflingers are known to be good driving ponies, but they certainly aren't known for flying through the air!"

"Don't worry," smiled Violet. "With a little help from the Rainbow Girls and the rainbow butterflies, Indigo will be perfect."

Evie looked up and saw that the sun was high in the sky.

"We haven't got much time," she said. "It's midday already."

"She's right, Violet," said Ginny. "You must go—after all, you can't delay the Rainbow Blossom Festival. I'll keep an eye on Corolla and her foal. They should be fine now."

Indigo took Evie, Violet, and Sparkles back to the yard, where all the Rainbow Girls were waiting for them with their baskets of delicate blossoms. They had had no idea why Corolla wasn't harnessed and ready to take them through the sky.

The girls were amazed and overjoyed to hear the news that Corolla had safely delivered a rainbow foal.

"It's so exciting!" said Rosa. "A new foal, born on the day of the

Rainbow Blossom Festival."

The Rainbow Girls couldn't wait to meet the new addition, but first they had a very important task—to prepare Indigo for the sprinkling of the blossoms. Evie and Violet carefully harnessed Indigo and adjusted the straps so that it fitted her perfectly.

"Now all you need is a pair of

wings!" smiled Violet, stroking Indigo's mane. "It won't hurt at all, but it will take some magic."

Sparkles's whiskers trembled and Evie let out a gasp when they heard this. The Rainbow Girls stood around Indigo, and without a word they reached into their pockets and took out their precious stones. The stones glittered and glowed in the spring sunshine. Violet whispered into the pony's ear and then placed her sparkling amethyst in Indigo's browband. Next, Rosa whispered something to Indigo and placed a dazzling ruby into her band. Evie wasn't sure what the Rainbow Girls were saying to her pony, but Indigo listened intently.

When the final jewel had been placed

into Indigo's bridle, the Rainbow Girls held hands in their circle and looked up to the sky. A swirl of rainbow butterflies fluttered and spiraled around Indigo until they almost hid her from view. All that Evie and Sparkles could see was Indigo's calm face.

When the butterflies stopped spiraling and flew away, Evie and Sparkles were astounded by what they

saw. Indigo stood proudly showing off the most magnificent pair of butterfly wings, with shimmering pink swirls and pale yellow whorls. Indigo shook herself and stretched her wings out in the sun. Evie saw that around the edge of each wing were tiny amethysts, rubies, and other twinkling gemstones.

"Hooray!" said Violet. "We did it!

What a gorgeous rainbow pony you are, Indigo."

Evie ran over and gave her beautiful pony a big hug and a stroke.

"Come on, girls," said Rosa. "We've no time to lose!"

Violet and Evie attached the chariot to Indigo's harness. They gave Indigo a few minutes to get used to it and then carefully loaded up the chariot with the baskets of delicate blossoms. Finally, they were ready to go.

"All aboard!" said Rosa, smiling.

Everyone climbed into the chariot and took their positions. Violet held the reins at the front of the chariot and made sure there was enough room for Evie beside her. Sparkles was feeling a bit nervous, so he snuggled up into Evie's arms.

"All right, Indigo," called Violet. "You know what you need to do. Just take your time and you'll be fine."

Indigo walked out of the stable yard into the field where all the butterflies were waiting. She broke into a fast trot, and when she moved to a smooth canter, Evie realized that her hooves were no longer touching the ground. Indigo was flying!

The butterflies fluttered around the Rainbow Garden and the chariot followed silently, pulled along by the magnificent Indigo. Evie and Sparkles looked out and saw they weren't too high in the sky.

"Here's the first tree coming up!" called Rosa. "It's an apple!"

Magenta passed around the basket of creamy blossoms with a touch of

yellow around their frilly edges, and everyone took a handful.

"On the count of three," called Rosa. "One, two, three!"

Everyone opened their hands and let the blossoms flutter down. When the blossoms landed on the apple tree, they magically attached themselves to the branches, making the tree come to life with the promise of spring. The next tree was a cherry tree. Everyone

sprinkled it with blossoms that were painted with different shades of pink.

"I can't wait to come back at the end of the summer and see all the cherries," said Rosa as they flew on to the next tree.

Violet turned to Evie. "Would you like to have a go at driving Indigo?"

"Do you think I could?" asked Evie.

"Of course," said Violet, smiling. "You and Indigo are a great team."

Evie took the reins and immediately felt Indigo's power. Her wings were beating rhythmically and with every beat, Evie could feel the chariot being pulled farther through the air. The butterflies were guiding Indigo, so all Evie had to do was let her pony know that she was there for her.

CHAPTER 6

What's in a Name?

They flew around the Rainbow Garden, decorating each of the trees with their beautiful, handmade blossoms, and soon the garden was complete.

Evie and Sparkles loved flying through the air with the Rainbow Girls. The fresh spring air made Sparkles's fur tingle and Evie's cheeks turn rosy.

"This is amazing!" laughed Evie.

"Indigo is fantastic at pulling this chariot," said Violet. "And she looks as if she is enjoying herself too."

Violet was right. Indigo's ears were forward and she held her head up high as her rainbow mane flew out behind her. Princess Evie felt very proud of her.

"It's time for us to land now, Indigo," called Violet. "But don't worry, the butterflies will guide you."

Evie felt her pony descend as the butterflies led them to a clearing in the garden. Indigo's wings slowed down and soon she was trotting through the grass. Everyone cheered as she came to a halt.

"That was a perfect landing," said Rosa, opening the chariot's door and helping everyone out.

Azure and Fern took a large picnic basket out of the chariot and together the Rainbow Girls laid out the special feast.

"I should think you're hungry after all that flying, Indigo," said Violet as Indigo tucked into the grass. "You're probably thirsty too. We'll get you some fresh water."

Violet and Evie went over to the garden's magic well and pulled out a bucket of fresh, clear water. The friends released the chariot from Indigo's harness and loosened some of the straps so the pony could relax.

They walked over to the picnic blanket, which was spread out beneath a fluttering cherry tree, and joined Sparkles. He was sitting with the Rainbow Girls and already enjoying some special kitten biscuits.

"What a feast!" said Evie when she saw all the plates of delicious food that Azure and Fern had prepared.

"Help yourself!" said Azure. "There's plenty for everyone."

Evie took a plate and filled it with an assortment of scrumptious sandwiches and delicious dips, as well as passion-fruit parcels and tasty tarts filled with tiny apricots and almonds. Azure and Fern poured everyone a glass of rose-petal lemonade. Then Rosa and Violet stood up.

"We would like to propose a toast to Princess Evie, Sparkles, and Indigo," said Rosa.

"We'd like to thank you for coming back to the Rainbow Garden, Evie," added Violet. "And especially for helping to save our special day!"

All the Rainbow Girls raised their glasses and toasted Evie, Sparkles, and Indigo.

"It's certainly been an adventure!" laughed Evie. "Perhaps we should toast the health of Corolla and her foal too."

"Of course!" agreed Rosa.

Everyone raised their glasses of rose-petal lemonade and wished Corolla and her newborn foal good health.

"We'll have to think of a name for the foal," said Violet.

"I know," said Magenta. "How about Blossom?"

"Or perhaps Kaleidoscope!" added Rosa.

"That's a lovely name, but it might be too long," said Violet. "We could call her Cherry."

"Or Rainbow," suggested Azure.

The Rainbow Girls had lots of ideas, and the discussion continued as the girls tidied up the plates and the remainder of the picnic. Sparkles, bored by all this, played with a heart-shaped petal that had floated down from a branch above. A gentle breeze blew it out of his paws' reach every time he got close to catching it. After a few minutes of chasing, the pretty petal landed on his nose.

Violet and Evie began to giggle when they saw his cute little petal-nose. The other Rainbow Girls turned to see what was so funny.

"That's brilliant, Sparkles!" said Violet. "We could call the new foal Petal."

Everyone agreed that the name Petal was just right.

"What a clever cat you are, Sparkles," said Evie, giving her kitten a big hug and blowing the pretty petal away.

"I think we should have the naming ceremony before you go," said Violet.

"What an excellent idea!" said Rosa.

CHAPTER 7

Rainbow Wishes

Before they went to the field on the edge of Kaleidoscope Wood, the girls made little crowns and garlands using the pretty blossoms that were left over in the baskets.

Evie and Violet took off Indigo's harness. They wove cherry blossoms into her mane and draped a garland of peach blossoms around her neck. Rosa even made Sparkles a crown of tiny hawthorn blossoms. Everyone looked beautiful, and soon they were ready to see Corolla and Petal.

When they got to the yard, Violet went to the feed shed and got Corolla a scoop of oats to keep her strength up. Ginny took them to see the mare and her new foal. The rainbow foal's coat shimmered and Corolla looked content.

"They are doing really well," the vet smiled.

"We've come to perform a naming

ceremony, Ginny," said Violet. "Would you help us?"

"Of course," said Ginny. "What have you decided to call her?"

"Petal," said Violet.

"Sparkles chose it," said Rosa.

"What a pretty name," said Ginny. "It's perfect for such a pretty foal."

The little foal was very inquisitive when she saw the Rainbow Girls and was especially interested in Sparkles. They touched noses and Sparkles purred while Petal whickered. Corolla was pleased to see everyone and neighed happily when Violet gave her the bucket of oats. Evie gently draped a garland of blossoms around Corolla's neck and tucked a little spray of flowers into Petal's mane. Now they were all ready for the ceremony.

Everyone stood around Corolla and Petal and, as if by magic, a rainbow appeared above them.

"We are here today to celebrate the safe arrival of Corolla's foal," said Ginny. "A foal is full of promise and each one of us here will help to take care of her and love her. We give her

the name Petal and will each give her a wish for her future."

"Petal, I wish you happiness in the Rainbow Kingdom," said Violet.

"Petal, I wish you fields full of fresh grass," said Rosa.

"Petal, I wish you many safe journeys through the sky," said Magenta.

Princess Evie hadn't been sure what was going to happen, but after listening to Violet, Rosa, and Magenta,

she realized what she had to do.

She looked at the little foal and thought about all the amazing things that had happened that day. She thought about returning to the Rainbow Garden to see her old friends, about finding the foal, and about Indigo pulling the jeweled chariot through the sky.

"Petal, I wish you many, many wonderful adventures shared with friends."

Each of the Rainbow Girls and Ginny gave Petal a wish, while Corolla looked on proudly.

"We'd better take Corolla and Petal back to the shelter by the yard," said Violet when they had all finished. "It looks as if it's going to rain soon."

A dark cloud moved slowly toward them.

"I think it's time to make our way back to Starlight Stables," said Evie. "Indigo could do with some rest after today's excitement—we all could!"

Sparkles rubbed up against Evie's ankle and meowed.

"Thank you, Indigo, for coming back to see us," said Rosa, stroking Indigo's rainbow mane. "And for pulling our chariot through the sky. You saved the day!"

"Well done, Sparkles, for choosing the perfect name for Corolla's foal," said Ginny, as she cuddled the kitten.

"And thank you for helping me with Corolla," said Violet, giving Evie a big hug.

"That's what friends are for," smiled Evie. "We promise we'll come back to visit you as soon as we can."

"We'd love to see you all soon," said Violet. "You must come back for next year's Rainbow Blossom Festival. Corolla and Indigo could pull the chariot together."

Everyone waved as Indigo trotted off to the tunnel of trees. They didn't have far to go because the tunnel was just in Kaleidoscope Wood. Princess Evie knew that Indigo's beautiful wings would disappear when they came out of the tunnel and were back at Starlight Stables. She stroked them one last time.

"You are a very beautiful rainbow pony, Indigo," said Evie.

Indigo shook her mane and happily went into the tunnel. When they came out, her coat had returned to its beautiful gold and, of course, her wings had disappeared.

All of Princess Evie's ponies called out to them, welcoming them back to the stables. Evie took off Indigo's tack and groomed her, checking her for any strains or injuries.

"Well done," said Evie. "You worked

hard today. You are such a strong pony—and a magic one too!"

Indigo nuzzled up to Evie. She loved going through the tunnel of trees and having adventures with Evie and Sparkles.

When Evie turned her Haflinger pony out into the paddock, Indigo rolled on the ground and then trotted around the field with her friends Silver and Willow. Evie and Sparkles went into the tack room to hang up Indigo's bridle and saddle.

"We'll have to carry on with our spring-cleaning tomorrow, Sparkles," said Evie. "There's lots more tack to oil, but I'm just too tired to do it today."

Sparkles was sitting by the hook for Indigo's bridle, looking up at

something that was hanging from it. Princess Evie carefully put Indigo's tack down and went over to see what it could be.

"Well, I never!" she said, smiling. "It looks as if Indigo is going to have lots of fun this spring. It's a driving harness, Sparkles!"

Evie took the harness down carefully. It was beautiful, with silver buckles and tiny gemstones sparkling along the reins.

"Thank you, Rainbow Girls," said

Evie. "What an unforgettable day."

Evie and Sparkles made their way back to Starlight Castle. They decided to walk through the fruit orchard, and as they did, they noticed something amazing.

"Look, Sparkles!" said Evie, pointing to the branches.

All the trees were covered with fluffy blossoms.

"Meow," said Sparkles as he began to chase a pink cherry-blossom petal that was floating on the spring breeze.

"I'm sure they weren't there this morning," laughed Evie. "I think that the springtime magic has really started!"

Pony Facts & Activities

Evie

LIVES AT:
Starlight Castle

FAVORITE FOOD:
Apple-blossom ice cream

FAVORITE PASTIME:
Going on adventures with magic ponies

FAVORITE FLOWER:
Violets

FANTASY JOB:
Training unicorns for the Olympics

Indigo

BREED:
Haflinger pony

FEATURES:
Very strong, quick learners, very friendly, driving ponies

HEIGHT:
From thirteen hands to fifteen hands

COLOR:
All shades of chestnut with light-colored manes and tails

Horse Tack

Tack is the name for all the equipment you use to ride a pony. Can you guess what the piece of equipment is from the description?

1. The rider sits on this.
2. This goes in the pony's mouth and is connected to number 4.
3. The rider holds these in their hands and uses them to steer the pony.
4. This goes over the head of the pony and connects numbers 2 and 3.
5. The rider's feet go into these.
6. This sits under number 1 to protect the pony's back.

ANSWERS: 1. SADDLE 2. BIT 3. REINS 4. BRIDLE 5. STIRRUPS 6. SADDLE PAD

Birthstones

The Rainbow Girls each have a special magic stone that they use to help Indigo fly. Every month has a specific stone associated with it. Which one is your special stone?

January—Garnet
This red stone is a symbol of love and compassion.

February—Amethyst
This pretty purple stone is said to help people have pleasant dreams.

March—Aquamarine
This stone is usually a pale blue-green color and can help encourage bravery.

April—Diamond
This very expensive stone is beautifully clear and sparkly. It is often used in wedding or engagement rings.

May—Emerald
A beautiful green color, this stone is quite rare and is said to bring wisdom if you wear it.

June—Moonstone
A very lucky stone that is supposed to bring good fortune! This stone can be different colors: sometimes milky-white and sometimes almost blue.

July—Ruby
This is another beautiful red stone, sometimes used to protect against bad dreams.

August—Peridot
This stone is quite unusual but is a very pretty green color. It is supposed to help bring happiness to the wearer.

September—Sapphire
This stunning blue stone helps you to think through difficult problems.

October—Opal
This can be lots of different colors and sometimes looks transparent. It's often described as a stone of inspiration and creativity.

November—Topaz
A pretty stone that comes in many colors. Yellow topaz is said to be a symbol of love and affection.

December—Turquoise
This stone is bright blue and a symbol of friendship and peace.

Make a Butterfly Garland

The Rainbow Garden butterflies helped guide Indigo through the trees in the Rainbow Blossom Festival. Follow these steps to craft a butterfly garland to decorate your space and make it as pretty as the butterflies in the festival.

What you'll need:
A few sheets of paper (It can be plain, colored, or even patterned.)
A piece of thin cardboard
A pencil
A pair of scissors
A glue stick
Some strong thread or thin ribbon

To create your butterflies:

1. Find a small or medium-sized butterfly shape that you like, and copy it onto the cardboard. Cut this out to get your template.
2. Using the template, trace the shape onto your paper, and cut it out. You will need twice as many butterflies as you want on your garland.
3. Feel free to decorate the shapes with colored pencils or markers.

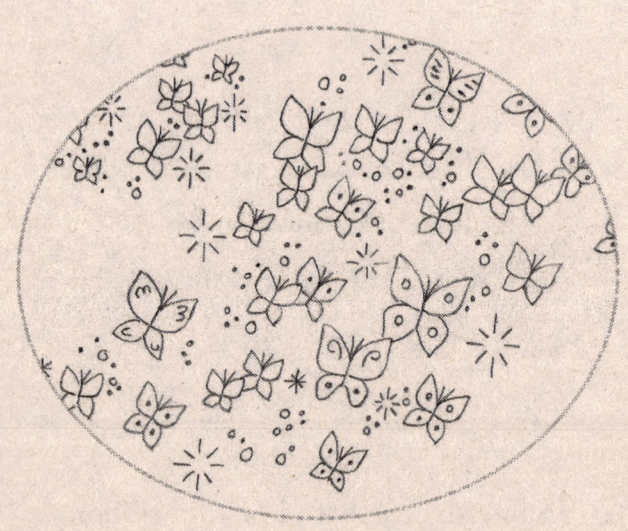

To create the garland:

1. Cut your thread or ribbon to the desired length of the garland. Tie a loop at each end for hanging.
2. Place your first butterfly facedown on a flat surface, and use your glue stick to draw a big X shape across the wings. Then add an extra line of glue down the midline where the wings meet.
3. Find the middle of your thread or ribbon, and lay it across the midline of your glued butterfly shape. Then lay another butterfly shape faceup on top of it, and press firmly.
4. Repeat this process along your ribbon, spacing the butterfly shapes as evenly as possible. Be sure all of your butterfly shapes are pointed in the same direction.
5. Decorate! Drape your garland across a window, in a doorway, on a wall, or wherever you want your butterflies.

Pegasus Facts

Corolla is a very different type of pony from Evie's, as she has wings! The most famous winged horse was Pegasus, who appeared in Greek myths. He was said to be a beautiful winged horse and the son of Poseidon, the god of the sea. There were many stories told about Pegasus, but one of the most famous was that he became the great friend of the king of the gods, Zeus. They were such good friends that Zeus turned Pegasus into a constellation of stars so that he could live forever. Pegasus was supposed to have many magical powers, including being able to stop a mountain from growing any taller by kicking it. As a friend of Zeus, he also carried Zeus's thunderbolts through the sky.

READ & LEARN
with *simon kids*

Keep your child reading, learning, and having fun with Simon Kids!

A one-stop shop where you can **find downloadable resources, watch interactive author videos, browse books by reading level, and more!**

**Visit us at
SimonandSchusterPublishing.com/ReadandLearn/**

And follow us @SimonKids

 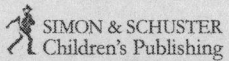 

SIMON & SCHUSTER
Children's Publishing

Looking for another great book?
Find it
IN THE MIDDLE.

Fun, fantastic books for kids
in the in-be**TWEEN** age.

IntheMiddleBooks.com

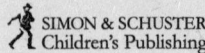 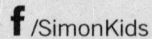 /SimonKids 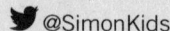 @SimonKids

Unicorn Riding Camp

For Pip & Jess, xx
—*SARAH KILBRIDE*

To Agnieszka
—*SOPHIE TILLEY*

If you purchased this book without a cover, you should be aware that this book is stolen property. It was reported as "unsold and destroyed" to the publisher, and neither the author nor the publisher has received any payment for this "stripped book."

This book is a work of fiction. Any references to historical events, real people, or real places are used fictitiously. Other names, characters, places, and events are products of the author's imagination, and any resemblance to actual events or places or persons, living or dead, is entirely coincidental.

ALADDIN
An imprint of Simon & Schuster Children's Publishing Division
1230 Avenue of the Americas, New York, New York 10020
First Aladdin paperback edition June 2021
Text copyright © 2014 by Sarah KilBride
Cover illustration copyright © 2021 by Paula Franco
Interior illustrations based on artwork originated by Sophie Tilley copyright © 2014
Originally published in Great Britain in 2014 by Simon & Schuster UK Ltd.
Also available in an Aladdin hardcover edition.
All rights reserved, including the right of reproduction in whole or in part in any form.
ALADDIN and related logo are registered trademarks of Simon & Schuster, Inc.
For information about special discounts for bulk purchases, please contact
Simon & Schuster Special Sales at 1-866-506-1949 or business@simonandschuster.com.
The Simon & Schuster Speakers Bureau can bring authors to your live event. For more information or to book an event contact the Simon & Schuster Speakers Bureau
at 1-866-248-3049 or visit our website at www.simonspeakers.com.
Cover designed by Tiara Iandiorio
The text of this book was set in Sabon LT Std.
Manufactured in the United States of America 0421 OFF
2 4 6 8 10 9 7 5 3 1
Library of Congress Cataloging-in-Publication Data
Names: KilBride, Sarah, author. | Tilley, Sophie, illustrator.
Title: Unicorn riding camp / Sarah KilBride ; interior illustrations by Sophie Tilley.
Description: New York : Aladdin, 2021. | Series: Princess Evie ; 2 | Audience: Ages 6 to 9. |
Summary: Princess Evie's magical pony Diamond transforms into a unicorn during Unicorn Riding Camp in Cloud Kingdom where they help a runaway unicorn and her cloud sprite rider find their way back home.
Identifiers: LCCN 2020051867 (print) | LCCN 2020051868 (ebook) |
ISBN 9781534476318 (hardcover) | ISBN 9781534476301 (paperback) |
ISBN 9781534476325 (ebook)
Subjects: CYAC: Princesses—Fiction. | Horsemanship—Fiction. |
Unicorns—Fiction. | Fairies—Fiction.
Classification: LCC PZ7.1.K5464 Un 2021 (print) | LCC PZ7.1.K5464 (ebook) |
DDC [Fic]—dc23
LC record available at https://lccn.loc.gov/2020051867
LC ebook record available at https://lccn.loc.gov/2020051868

Princess EVIE

By Sarah KilBride

Interior illustrations by Sophie Tilley

Unicorn Riding Camp

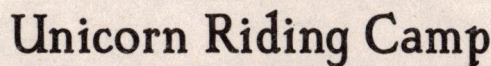

ALADDIN
NEW YORK   LONDON   TORONTO   SYDNEY   NEW DELHI

CHAPTER 1
A Sunny Start

CHAPTER 2
Away to Unicorn Stables

CHAPTER 3
Unicorn Camp Chaos

CHAPTER 4
Raphaela's Magic

CHAPTER 5
The Rescue Party

CHAPTER 6
Home and Dry

CHAPTER 7
Team Cloud Sprite

CHAPTER 1

A Sunny Start

"What a perfect day, Diamond!" said Princess Evie as she trotted through the gates of Starlight Stables.

Even though it was early, the sun was scorching. It was much hotter in the stable yard than on the top of the Golden Mountain, where they had enjoyed a lovely, cool breeze. The bright morning sun made Evie's Connemara pony's coat gleam.

"I think your friends are pleased to see you, Diamond!"

Evie was right. All her lovely ponies were trotting to the gate, neighing, squealing, and welcoming Diamond back.

It wasn't only Evie's ponies that were glad to see them. Evie's little kitten, Sparkles, skipped over to the tie post and rubbed against Evie's ankle.

"We've just had the most amazing ride," Evie said with a smile. "The Golden Mountain is ever so high. At first we were surrounded by mountain clouds, but they soon cleared and then we could see for miles."

Diamond was the perfect pony for mountain rides. She had great stamina and was very strong. Of course, Evie loved riding all her ponies, especially on summer days like these. But Evie's ponies weren't any old ponies—they were magic ponies. Whenever Evie rode them through the tunnel of trees, they took her on magical adventures in faraway lands.

Evie's ponies were transformed the moment they came out of the tunnel. For instance, when Neptune galloped out onto a beach, her coat became the color of the sparkling ocean. And that wasn't the only magic that happened—Evie's clothes changed too! She loved the beautiful new outfits she wore on their adventures. When she went to the North Pole with the snow fairies, she wore a gorgeous fluffy pink cloak and warm boots. Evie looked up at the cloudless sky—it was hard to imagine snow today!

Evie checked to see if Diamond had cooled down, especially where the saddle had been and under Diamond's elbows and hind legs. Because Diamond's breathing had slowed down to normal, Evie could now give her some fresh water and brush out her shining coat.

"You've worked hard this morning, Diamond, climbing up that steep mountain and galloping along the ridge."

Evie went into the tack room to get her grooming kit and Sparkles padded in after her. It wasn't just Diamond who was hot. Evie had been out in the sun for quite some time, and the tack room felt lovely and cool. The walls were lined with saddles, bridles, and, of course, rosettes. Evie walked toward the metal trunk where she kept her grooming kit. As her eyes adjusted to the shadows of the tack room, she noticed something.

"Have we had visitors this morning, Sparkles?"

Sparkles meowed. Of course he couldn't talk—he was only a cat, but Evie was positive that he could understand every word she said.

"I think someone's been here while I was out on the mountain. Look!"

Evie pointed to the metal trunk and Sparkles hopped up for a closer inspection.

There, leaning against a bottle of hoof oil, was a golden envelope.

"Who's it from?" asked Evie.

Sparkles sniffed the envelope and then looked at Evie, blinking patiently.

"You're right—there's only one way to find out!"

Evie picked the envelope up and took out the letter. As she read it, she smiled.

"Come on, Sparkles, I have to read this to Diamond!" And they raced out to the sunny yard with the letter.

Dear Evie,

How are things at Starlight Stables? I hope you're enjoying this lovely summer with all your gorgeous ponies—fantastic riding weather, isn't it?

I'm writing to you because I wondered if you and Diamond would like to come to the Cloud Kingdom and join our Unicorn Riding Camp. It starts today and should be great fun. There'll be lots of cloud sprites there, and there'll be lots of lessons and activities to help us learn all about our unicorns. Just leave your kit in the stable yard and I'll send a cloud to pick it up. I'll be waiting for you on the clouds when you come out of the tunnel of trees.

Really hope you can make it—it would be wonderful to see you and Diamond again.
Lots of love,
Skye xxxxxx
PS: PLEASE bring Sparkles too xxxxxxx
PPS: Please give all your ponies a hug from me.
PPPS: PLEASE give Sparkles an extra-special hug too!!!!

Diamond neighed. She loved taking Evie away on adventures, and Unicorn Riding Camp certainly sounded very exciting. Diamond and Evie had shared an amazing adventure the last time they'd visited the Cloud Kingdom. They had competed in the Unicorn Games and had even won first prize in the obstacle race!

There was no time to lose. Evie raced into the tack room to pack. She found the special riding gloves that Skye had given her, embroidered with little gold unicorns. Then she checked her grooming kit, making sure that everything was clean and in good condition.

"How thrilling—we're going to see Skye and her magic unicorn, Jewel, again," said Evie as she took her backpack of useful things down from its peg. "I can't wait!"

She carried her kit out into the yard.

"Skye said to leave our kit here," said Evie. "I wonder if that's the cloud that's going to take it to the Cloud Kingdom?"

The blue sky had been clear a moment ago, but now there was a large white cloud floating over the Golden Mountain. As it came toward Starlight Castle, it floated lower and lower, drifting past the turrets and over the gardens. By the time it arrived at Starlight Stables, it was skimming along the ground.

Sparkles jumped up into Evie's arms—he'd never seen anything quite like this before! The cloud came toward them and for a few seconds they couldn't see a thing, then it floated back up into the sky.

"Look at that!" said Evie.

There was just an empty space where her kit box had been.

"Hop up, Sparkles. It's time to go to the Cloud Kingdom!" said Evie as she put on her backpack of useful things. "I think our luggage will be there before us!"

Evie and Sparkles mounted Diamond, and soon they were galloping toward the tunnel of trees. Evie closed her eyes and took a deep breath.

CHAPTER 2

Away to Unicorn Stables

When Evie opened her eyes, the Cloud Kingdom stretched out around them for miles. The sunshine made the clouds glitter with pretty pastel colors. Diamond's coat shimmered with the same soft colors and she now had a magnificent golden unicorn's horn that sparkled in the sunshine. Evie looked down and saw that she was wearing a stylish riding jacket embroidered with fine gold thread, a pair of jodhpurs, and gleaming riding boots.

"I think we're ready for Unicorn Camp," she whispered as they trotted out onto the soft, fluffy clouds.

"You certainly are!" called a friendly voice.

It was Skye. The cloud sprite appeared from the shimmering mist on her beautiful unicorn, Jewel. Her pretty vest was edged with daisies and her pale pink jodhpurs were decorated with silver thread.

"Skye!" Evie said with a laugh. "How lovely to see you."

Jewel whinnied, and Diamond and Jewel touched noses and said their unicorn hellos.

"I'm so pleased you could make it, Evie," said Skye.

"We wouldn't have missed Unicorn Riding Camp for the world!" said Evie.

"Are you ready for a gallop, Diamond?" asked Skye.

Diamond neighed and tossed her sparkling mane.

"Follow me, Evie! We'll be there in no time," said Skye.

Skye turned her unicorn around and broke into a fast trot, a canter, and then a gallop. Diamond didn't need

any encouragement to follow and soon they were racing along the clouds. Evie could feel her cheeks glow as the wind whistled past.

They sped through puffy white clouds that splashed the girls with rainbow drops. They sailed over great powdery plains and jumped across small pink

clouds that patterned the sky like stepping stones.

Normally when Diamond galloped, Evie could hear her pony's hooves on the ground, but Diamond was galloping along silently with her glittering mane flying. Evie remembered that a unicorn's hooves never make a sound—it was one of the magical things about them.

Skye was right; it wasn't long before they were at the gate of the riding school in the clouds.

"This is where they train the Unicorn Olympic Team," said Skye excitedly. "I've always dreamed about riding here."

The friends dismounted, landing softly. Evie thought that walking on clouds felt a little like walking on snow. Her feet gently sank, leaving little prints. Skye opened the beautiful golden gate.

"We'll take our unicorns to the stables first and get them settled in," she said. "Then it'll be time to go to the Great Hall to meet the instructors."

As they led their unicorns into the yard they spotted a map pinned on to a post. A little cloud sprite was looking at it. She

turned and called over to the friends.

"What are your unicorns' names?"

"My unicorn is called Diamond," replied Evie. "And this is Jewel."

"You're in stables eleven and twelve and we're in stable thirteen." She smiled at her unicorn. "Unlucky for some!"

She turned to take her unicorn to

the stable block when two other cloud sprites arrived and trotted silently across the yard on their unicorns, almost knocking her down.

"Watch where you're going!" shouted one rider, who had a long golden braid.

The little cloud sprite was too stunned to say anything. The riders smirked at her as she stood with her mouth open.

"You'll catch flies if you stay like that!" said the rider with the long braid. She checked the map and the other rider giggled.

"Come on, let's go and make ourselves at home," said the first rider. "We're in stables fourteen and fifteen."

They trotted off to find their stables.

"They're going to be our neighbors,"

the little sprite said to her unicorn. "I told you thirteen was unlucky for some."

"Are you all right?" asked Evie.

Tears had begun to well up in the little sprite's eyes.

"I'm fine."

"I'm sorry—we should have stuck up for you," said Evie.

"It's a good thing you didn't," said the sprite, looking down at her scuffed riding boots. "They're the Sunshine Girls, and you don't want to get on the wrong side of them. I met them at last year's camp. It's best to keep out of their way."

The little cloud sprite turned and led her unicorn away.

"What's your name?" Skye called after her, but she had already disappeared around the corner, taking her unicorn to her stable.

"Let's have a look at the list," said Evie as she scanned the map. "Here we are. She's called Wanda and her unicorn is Zephyr. I wonder if she has any friends at the camp."

"Well, I think we should be her friends. That's what camp is all about," said Skye. "Let's keep an eye on her and make sure that the Sunshine Girls don't try picking on her again."

Evie and Skye led Diamond and Jewel to their stables, where their grooming kits were waiting for them.

"I told you they'd be here before us, Diamond!" said Evie.

"We're across from Wanda," Skye said with a smile.

"And the Sunshine Girls," added Evie.

The riders who had just been so rude to Wanda were now busily settling their unicorns in. They were making quite a lot of noise about it—singing and shouting, shrieking with laughter and chasing each other around.

"They look like they're having fun," said Evie as she gently put her hand on Diamond's muzzle.

She could feel her unicorn getting

twitchy and knew that Diamond didn't like all this noise.

"Let's get our unicorns settled," said Skye. "We need to be in the Great Hall for the introduction to camp in half an hour. If we team up with Wanda, we'll get it done quickly."

So Evie and Skye went to Wanda's

stable and introduced themselves. Soon they were busy helping one another.

Wanda collected some golden apples from the barrel in the yard while Skye filled three buckets with fresh water. Evie and Sparkles went to the barn to collect some straw for their unicorns' bedding. They needed a whole bale, but the bales were too heavy for Evie to pick up on her own.

"Do you need a hand?" asked a kind voice.

Evie turned around. Standing behind her was the most beautiful cloud sprite she had ever seen. Light seemed to shine from her sky-blue eyes and soft curls floated around her face. She wore a pair of pale blue jodhpurs and her silk shirt had tiny pearl buttons.

"Come on," she said with a smile. "Let's go and find a wheelbarrow."

As they lifted the bale into an old wheelbarrow, Evie found out that the beautiful cloud sprite's name was Raphaela Plume and she was one of the camp's instructors.

"I used to come to Unicorn Camp when I was younger," said Raphaela. "I hope you have as much fun as I did!"

Evie smiled—then she remembered the Sunshine Girls. She hoped they weren't going to spoil things.

The wheelbarrow wobbled all over the place, and by the time they got back to the stable, Raphaela and Evie were giggling.

Evie introduced her new friend to Skye and Wanda, but the cloud sprites didn't say hello or even smile. They just went red!

"See you at the meeting!" said Raphaela.

She waved and headed off toward the Great Hall. Wanda and Skye stared after her, speechless. Even the Sunshine

Girls had stopped messing around and were staring at the lovely sprite as she disappeared around the corner.

"I don't believe it!" gasped Skye. "Raphaela Plume—the most famous Olympic gold medalist in the Cloud Kingdom."

"She was chatting and laughing with you, Evie, like a normal sprite!" said Wanda.

"Well, she is normal," said Evie. "Not like you two—staring at her and not saying a word!"

"You don't understand, Evie," said Wanda. "She is the most fabulous unicorn rider in the entire Cloud Kingdom!"

"I hope she's going to teach us some of her riding secrets," said Skye. "Oh, this is going to be such an amazing camp!"

She did an excited little jump into the air.

"Come on, you two, before you get

any giddier!" said Evie as she picked Sparkles up. "We've got five minutes to get to the Great Hall for our meeting."

CHAPTER 3

Unicorn Camp Chaos

The Great Hall was on an enormous cloud. Sparkles led the way along the path that followed the soft curves of the cloud. As they climbed the steps, the hall's magnificent door magically opened.

"Look at that!" Evie gasped.

She pointed to the domed ceiling. It was painted with a beautiful skyscape of shimmering clouds. On one side of the dome, the morning sunrise was painted in warm colors. The evening

sky was on the opposite side. It was a deep blue that looked as if it went on forever, scattered with constellations of gold stars. The arched windows were open and pale blue curtains floated gently in the breeze.

A little crowd of sprites was already waiting, and the air was full of chattering and laughter. Clouds the size of plates floated from sprite to sprite, carrying tasty marshmallows, pink cotton candy on cocktail sticks, and tiny fairy cakes that were so fluffy they almost floated away! Whenever a plate began to look empty, it magically filled up with more treats.

Skye and Wanda met a few sprites they knew, and Evie recognized Rosy from when she, Diamond, and Sparkles had taken part in the Unicorn Games. Rosy smiled and waved as she came over to say hello. Then the huge wooden doors at the end of the hall opened and in walked three important-looking cloud sprites.

"The instructors," whispered Skye. "Look! There's Raphaela."

"I hope we don't get Professor Nimbus first," said Wanda. "She's the one on the left. She trains riders for the Olympic team."

Evie could feel poor Sparkles jump when the professor began to speak.

"Welcome to this year's Unicorn Riding Camp," said Professor Nimbus. "I hope all your unicorns have settled in. This afternoon I will be teaching the training session on riding technique."

"I am Madam Mariposa," said the older, shorter sprite, who was standing beside the professor. She had a warm smile and fluffy white hair that had a silver lining like a halo. "I will be helping you learn about unicorn well-being and stable management."

"And I'm going to be helping you bond with your unicorns," said Raphaela. "And together, we will develop your unicorn empathy skills."

There was a ripple of excitement among the cloud sprites.

"There will be a list of the groups on the noticeboard after lunch," said Professor Nimbus.

Evie spotted Professor Nimbus winking at the girl with the long blond braid before turning to leave.

"That's Professor Nimbus's niece," Rosy whispered in her ear. "Her name's Storm."

All the cloud sprites filed out of the Great Hall and followed the long corridor to the dining room.

The dining room was hung with paintings of unicorns and each of the round tables was lit with a golden candelabra. Everyone was hungry; it

had been a long morning and the room buzzed with anticipation. Wanda, Skye, and Evie shared a table and enjoyed the fluffy bread and hot soup. Dessert was the most delicious cake Evie had ever tasted—layers of light sponge with heavenly mousse in between.

"Imagine learning how to communicate with your unicorn like Raphaela does!" said Wanda when they

had all finished their lunch. Everyone was starting to leave the dining room to have a look at the list that had been pinned on to the noticeboard.

"Nonsense!" snorted Storm as she and her friend pushed past Wanda's chair. "My aunt says the only way to communicate with a unicorn is to show it who's the boss."

"Let's hope we're not in Storm's

group," said Wanda, and all the friends nodded.

"There's only one way to find out," said Evie. "Come on, let's go and have a look at the lists."

"Oh, this is so exciting," said Skye. "I hope we're all in the same group."

But they weren't. Skye had been put in Rosy's group.

"What a shame I'm not with you," said Skye.

PRINCESS EVIE
& DIAMOND

WANDA
& ZEPHYR

STORM
& MISTY

JUNO
& CHERUB

"It might have been a lucky escape, Skye," said Evie. "Look who's in our group."

Princess Evie & Diamond
Wanda & Zephyr
Storm & Misty
Juno & Cherub

"The Sunshine Girls," said Wanda.

"Never mind," said Skye. "They're probably lovely once you get to know them."

"Well, there's one good thing," said Evie, seeing that Wanda was looking a little worried. "Our first lesson is with Raphaela in the arena."

"Lucky you," said Skye. "I'm with Professor Nimbus."

The friends went off to saddle up their unicorns for the first lesson. But when they reached the stable yard, they were met with complete chaos. Cloud sprites were running about and shouting, trying to catch a unicorn that had escaped from her stable. She was rearing like a wild animal. When the unicorn was finally cornered by the sprites, the friends saw it was Zephyr—Wanda's unicorn.

"Zephyr!" shouted Wanda.

As soon as Zephyr heard Wanda's voice, she neighed, looking wildly around the yard for her owner.

"That animal is out of control!" said Storm, just as the instructors appeared. "Look at this mess."

"What's made Zephie do this?" asked Wanda, completely baffled by the scene of devastation.

The barrel of apples had been kicked over, straw was strewn across the yard,

water buckets had been knocked over, and some tack and a grooming kit lay in the big puddles.

"This is not acceptable," said Professor Nimbus, looking around the yard. "You will not join in any activities, Wanda, until you have cleaned this up. Is that clear?"

As the professor was talking,

Raphaela walked carefully toward Zephyr, murmuring quietly to the frightened unicorn. She helped Wanda put a halter on Zephyr and tied the unicorn up.

"Come along, everyone. Tack up, time for your first lesson," continued the professor.

As the other sprites tacked up, Wanda, Evie, and Skye looked at one another.

"There's no way you can be late for Professor Nimbus's lesson, Skye; she'll be annoyed," said Evie. "I'll help Wanda clear this up."

"I don't understand," said Wanda, looking at the stable door hanging off its hinges. "Zephyr has never done anything like this before. Why would she kick her door down?"

Evie and Wanda set about sweeping and cleaning the yard. Sparkles tried to cheer Wanda up by chasing after apples and catching straw that was blowing in the breeze, but the little sprite found it hard to smile.

"I just can't understand what got into Zephyr," she said.

CHAPTER 4

Raphaela's Magic

Wanda and Evie worked together to clear all the mess and were only ten minutes late for the start of their lesson. Storm and Juno were standing by their unicorns listening to Raphaela, who was resting her hand gently on her magnificent unicorn, Galaxy.

"Hey, sprites! I'm just giving a quick history of unicorns," said Raphaela. "The important thing to remember is, if you want your unicorn's trust, you must make them feel safe. When they

feel safe with you, they can relax and will let you lead—and that's when the magic begins!

"Our first exercise will help you get in tune with your unicorn. Every neigh, whinny, and squeal has a meaning, and the more you listen, the more you'll begin to understand. It all starts with the breath. Listen to your unicorn and copy her breathing."

The sprites and Evie stood closely by their unicorns. In a few moments, Evie and Diamond were almost touching noses and Wanda and Zephyr were leaning shoulder to shoulder. Juno and her unicorn were nodding heads in unison, with Juno giggling and Cherub whickering.

"It's great to see you share the same sense of humor, Juno!" said Raphaela.

"Ow!" yelped Storm. "Stop that now!"

Misty had been resting her head over Storm's shoulder and had started to nibble her fashionable riding jacket.

"Hold on, Storm."

Raphaela and Galaxy raced over to them. "She was telling you that she's your friend."

"Ruining my jacket is more like it," said Storm. "That's disgusting, Misty!"

Misty whinnied and shook her mane.

"Careful, Storm—that's not the way to speak to your unicorn," said Raphaela. "She's grooming you like a mother does to comfort her foal."

"I don't need to be comforted," snapped Storm.

"Well," replied Raphaela, "it seems your unicorn believes that you do."

Storm looked angry and turned away.

The next part of the lesson was what everyone had been looking forward to—developing unicorn empathy skills.

"Practice this on your unicorn, and one day you'll be able to calm and ride any unicorn in the Cloud Kingdom," Raphaela said.

"Stand close to your unicorn's midpoint. The midpoint is just by the withers, in front of your saddles. Stand quietly and try to feel your unicorn's beat. It's a cross between a pulse and a heartbeat," said Raphaela. "Let them feel your beat too."

Evie could feel Diamond's beat pulsing quietly and steadily. Diamond was standing so still and alert, Evie was sure that her unicorn was listening to hers. Next, Raphaela told the sprites to rest their arms over their unicorn's withers.

"Apply pressure so your unicorn

understands what's going to happen next," she said. "Once they steady themselves, it's time to hop up."

Everyone copied Raphaela as she demonstrated on her unicorn, Galaxy, and soon they were all up in the saddle. Everyone, that is, apart from Storm. Misty was still shifting her weight and hadn't yet settled, but instead of steadying her with the weight of her arm, Storm was pulling hard on her reins. This was making Misty raise her head and try to move away.

Raphaela rode over to Storm and let Galaxy gently breathe onto Misty's muzzle. The little unicorn relaxed and Storm was able to get up into the saddle.

The next task was to ride with loose reins. "I want you to practice going from a halt to a walk to a trot," said Raphaela. "Direct your unicorn by visualizing what you want her to do and where you want to go, and remember to talk to her."

The unicorns and their riders moved around the space. Soon, Wanda and

Zephyr were weaving in and out of some rainbow cones. Juno giggled as Cherub began to trot after a little cloud that had floated into the arena.

"Excellent, Juno; Cherub can sense that you like to play," said Raphaela.

Evie was amazed at how Diamond seemed to be able to read her mind. All she had to do was look in the direction she wanted to go, visualize turning, and Diamond would take the turn.

"This is such fun!" said Wanda, laughing as Zephyr jumped over a row of little sunbeams.

"How much longer?" asked Storm. "I can't wait till our next lesson so we can start learning useful stuff."

Her unicorn was standing by a rainbow jump and wouldn't budge.

"Try not to get angry," said Raphaela as Storm started to use her heels to try to make her unicorn move. "Perhaps it's time for a break—we've all been working hard."

Raphaela was giving Storm the chance to dismount and calm down, but Storm took no notice.

"Come on!" Storm shouted. "Move it!"

She smacked Misty's hindquarters and everyone gasped. Misty reared up high on her hind legs and let out a piercing neigh that made the other unicorns jump. Her nostrils flared and the whites of her eyes flashed wildly. Before anyone could take hold of Misty, she bolted over the arena's high fence and disappeared into a cloud.

Everyone watched in amazement and the air filled with squeals of panic from the unicorns.

The unicorns and their riders all knew the danger Storm was in as Misty, angry and frightened, took her into the Cloud Kingdom. "What on earth is going on here?" demanded Professor Nimbus, bursting into the arena.

Evie and the sprites looked at Raphaela. No one wanted to be the one to tell the angry professor what had happened to her niece. Raphaela looked uncomfortable, but she managed to explain.

"My niece is in terrible danger," said the professor. "The clouds are beginning to separate and a storm is brewing. How on earth could you have let this happen? That unicorn of hers doesn't need empathy; it needs discipline."

"Now isn't the time to discuss our differences," said Raphaela. "Our unicorns have a connection with Misty. I'll lead the group to find their friend and bring Storm back to safety."

"The Cloud Kingdom is a dangerous place. If we hear nothing from you within the hour, then I'll have no choice but to contact the Rainbow Rescue Team and tell them you have lost my niece."

The unicorns moved close together,

their noses almost touching. The riders waited, feeling the beats of their unicorns racing. Then the unicorns began to whicker—little noises that shivered out on their breath.

"They're talking," whispered Wanda.

"They're going to call to Misty," said Raphaela. "I hope that she can hear her friends."

Diamond raised her head, her unicorn horn glittering in the sun. She let out a neigh that Evie had never heard before. Evie could feel it travel through Diamond's body, starting at the top of her range. As it spiraled down, all the other unicorns in the circle joined in.

The unicorns' call seemed to go on for minutes, and as it went down to the lowest notes, all the unicorns at the camp had joined in. When it ended, everyone listened.

After a minute, out of the blue, came the sound everyone had been waiting for. It was Misty's reply, but it was coming from far, far away.

The unicorns pawed the ground, their ears forward, their horns glittering, and their eyes searching the horizon of clouds. Together, with their riders holding on tightly, they galloped out of the arena, through the yard and the golden gate, and onto the vast blanket of clouds.

"Slow down, everyone. The clouds are beginning to thin," said Raphaela.

She was right: little gaps were beginning to appear as some of the clouds began to float away. Evie could see glimpses of what lay beneath and felt Sparkles snuggling up close to her to be safe. If any of the unicorns lost their footing, it would be a long way down!

CHAPTER 5

The Rescue Party

Raphaela led them carefully in single file, scanning the clouds and making sure they rode a safe path. They kept their distance from any thinning clouds, and when they heard Misty neigh again, it was a little closer.

"Hooray!" said Juno. "We're on the right track."

"I hope Storm has managed to stay on," said Evie.

"She doesn't seem to get along very well with her unicorn," said Wanda.

"Storm has never been happy with Misty," said Juno. "She always thinks other sprites' rides are better than hers." Juno turned and looked apologetically at Wanda. "She wanted Zephyr and thought that if she made your unicorn look wild, you might want to get rid of her."

Everyone looked shocked. They all knew that pairing with a unicorn was for life.

"Get rid of Zephyr!" gasped Wanda.

"Was it Storm that broke Zephyr's door?" asked Raphaela.

"Yes," said Juno in a small voice.

"I knew Zephyr couldn't have done it." Wanda placed her hand on her unicorn's neck and pressed gently. "I never doubted you, Zephyr. I knew it wasn't you."

"You were with Storm when she turned this unicorn out of her stable and made that mess," said Raphaela. "Why would you stand by when she was being so cruel?"

"She's my friend," Juno said. "I know she was doing the wrong thing, but I feel sorry for her. She's been having a tough time."

"Feeling sorry for a friend who doesn't

know any better isn't enough," said Raphaela. "You need to be strong and help Storm do the right thing, even if that means risking losing her as a friend."

The procession fell silent. The clouds were darkening and a mist was beginning to form on them.

"Will the unicorns know their way back?" asked Juno.

"Only when the mist and the storm have cleared," said Raphaela.

"That might take longer than an hour," said Wanda, remembering Professor Nimbus was going to call the Rainbow Rescue Team.

Everyone knew that if they weren't back within an hour, Raphaela would be in a lot of trouble.

"We don't want to get caught in the storm," said Juno.

"Let me see if I've got anything that might help," said Evie. "I'm sure there's a compass in here."

She opened her backpack of useful things and, while she was looking, pulled out a pencil and a ball of red string. The instant Sparkles saw the string, he started to unravel it with his paws.

"You're brilliant, Sparkles!" said Evie. "We'll leave a trail of string and follow it on our way back."

Everyone felt better knowing they would be able to get back safely. They had traveled a long way from the Unicorn Riding Camp, and no one wanted to get caught in a cloud storm.

"What's that?" whispered Raphaela.

Everyone stopped and listened.

"Help!"

It was Storm shouting.

The search party hurried through the mist, following her calls. And there they were, Storm and Misty, stranded on an island of cloud. Evie could see the gap between their cloud and Storm's was widening. Storm was looking pale and Evie could see that Misty was trembling; they were both petrified.

"Help!" shouted Storm. "Help me!"

"The only one who can help you is

your unicorn," called over Raphaela. "Stay calm and try to remember what you learned this morning."

The only way Storm was going to be able to get off the cloud was if her unicorn could jump over the gap.

"Misty is a good jumper, Storm," called Juno. "Remember when she won the rainbow jumping at the Unicorn

Games? She can jump that gap easily."

Storm and Misty's cloud was floating farther away. If Misty was going to jump, she would have to do it quickly.

"Calm your unicorn with your breathing and soothe her with your words," Raphaela shouted across to Storm. "She has to trust you and feel safe."

Storm walked steadily to her unicorn's midpoint.

"Good girl, we'll be all right, just you see," Storm said, breathing slowly.

The unicorns, Evie, Sparkles, and all the sprites watched as Storm tried to calm her unicorn. Their little cloud island drifted away a bit more and Evie could see the huge drop below. It made her feel dizzy. Evie knew she'd be terrified if she had to make this jump.

Storm mounted Misty, and Evie was amazed to see that, for the first time, they looked like a riding pair.

"Well done, Storm," called Raphaela. "Now take your time and try to visualize Misty soaring through the air and landing safely, just like we did in the arena."

The pair stood still, and Storm closed

her eyes. When she opened them, Misty began to paw at the ground as if she couldn't wait, her eyes sparkling and her golden horn gleaming. The little unicorn reared up proudly and then began a fierce gallop toward the edge of the cloud.

They only had a short run-up before jumping. No one dared to breathe as the little unicorn flew into the air. She

sailed over the gap and landed silently not far from Evie, Sparkles, and Diamond.

Everyone cheered and whooped and neighed; the sound echoed through the clouds for miles around. "Thank you for saving us," said Storm as she leaned over to Raphaela and hugged her.

"It was you and your brave unicorn that did all the hard work," said

Raphaela. "I'm very proud of you."

"I'm very proud of Misty," said Storm, giving her unicorn a gentle hug. "I've been so hard on her. No wonder she wanted to run away from me!"

"I think she's seen another side of you," said Evie. "We all have."

Storm's face changed and her smile disappeared.

"There's something that I need to tell you, Wanda," she said, "about what happened in the yard after lunch."

"You can talk while we make our way back," said Raphaela. "We have to follow the red string and find the stables quickly."

"Before the storm starts," said Evie, looking at the dark clouds that had begun to hiss and spit.

Poor Sparkles hid under Evie's jacket! He hated thunder and could feel in his whiskers that the storm was about to start.

CHAPTER 6

Home and Dry

The unicorns followed the trail of red string, walking nose to tail through the crackling fog and storm clouds. Underneath their silent hooves the dark clouds rumbled. The cloudscape was changing fast. When they came to the end of the red string, Evie searched the horizon but the Unicorn Stables were nowhere to be seen.

After a few seconds, the sound of neighing filled the air.

"It's the other unicorns," said

Raphaela. "They're calling us back."

The unicorns pricked up their ears and neighed back to their friends joyfully. Before Evie and Sparkles knew it, Diamond and the other unicorns were racing over the snarling black clouds back to the stables. Soon they were in view.

"We've made it!" cheered Wanda.

Raphaela led Evie, Juno, Wanda, and Storm into the stable yard just as the first flash of lightning lit up the clouds beneath them, making the clouds shudder. All the other unicorns and riders welcomed the rescue party back, relieved and happy to be together again. Professor Nimbus and Madam Mariposa were standing at the front. As soon as the riders dismounted, Professor Nimbus rushed up to Storm.

"I'm so glad you're safe," she said, giving her niece a big hug. "I've been so worried."

"I'm all right," replied Storm, "thanks to Misty. You should have seen her jump. She was amazing!"

"Well, maybe you'll make the Olympic team after all!" said Professor Nimbus, stroking Misty's mane.

Storm told her aunt all about how she and Misty had been stranded on the cloud island. While she listened to

her niece, Professor Nimbus glared at Raphaela.

"Please don't be angry with Raphaela," said Storm as Raphaela led Galaxy to her stable. "I wouldn't have been able to get off that cloud without her help."

"Don't you worry yourself," said Professor Nimbus. "Just settle your unicorn and then come to the Great Hall. I'm sure you and your friends need some cake after all that excitement."

All the other cloud sprites had fed and groomed their unicorns, so Professor Nimbus took them to the Great Hall for tea. Juno, Wanda, Storm, and Evie took off their unicorns' tack, brushed out their coats, and helped them to recover from their

adventure with a gentle massage. The unicorns settled quickly and enjoyed the fresh water and hay that Skye and Madam Mariposa brought them.

"Well done for today," said Evie to Storm. "I never could have jumped over that gap. You and Misty are an amazing team."

"She's the best unicorn ever," said Storm, giving Misty a gentle hug.

"Your aunt seemed very proud of the way you rode today," said Madam Mariposa as she helped Storm brush out Misty's mane.

"I never thought my riding would be good enough for her," said Storm.

"Is that why you wanted a different unicorn?" asked Evie.

Storm looked embarrassed.

"I'm sorry, Misty," she said. "I thought you weren't as good as the other unicorns, but today I realized that it was me that was stopping us from being a team. I wouldn't bond with you, so you couldn't trust me."

"Trust is the key," said Madam Mariposa. "You learned that just in time, and it saved you and your unicorn from being lost in the sky."

"I'll never forget it," promised Storm. "It's not about being the boss like my aunt said—it's about getting to know each other, listening to each other, and being the best team you can be."

"That sounds like good advice," said Skye. "Not just for riders and their unicorns, but for friends too."

Storm smiled at them all and then took Wanda's hand.

"I know it won't make up for what I did," she said, "but I'm so sorry about the way I've treated you and Zephyr. I won't ever make the same mistake again."

"I'm so glad you're bonding with Misty," said Wanda. "You make a great team."

"I think we all make a great team," said Evie. And everyone cheered.

CHAPTER 7

Team Cloud Sprite

When all the unicorns were settled, Sparkles led Evie, Juno, Wanda, Skye, Storm, and Madam Mariposa to the dining room. As they followed the path, Madam Mariposa told them something about Raphaela and Professor Nimbus.

"Storm, your aunt used to love coming to Unicorn Riding Camp years ago," she said. "It was here that she met Raphaela and they became best friends. But after a few years they had to compete for a place on the Olympic team. Raphaela beat your aunt by a whisker in the finals, and Professor Nimbus never got over it or forgave her old friend."

"That's so sad. I wonder if they'll ever be able to be friends again," said Storm as they walked into the dining room. "I hope so. After all, Raphaela helped me bond with Misty!"

"It looks like they might have started," said Wanda.

She was right; Professor Nimbus and Raphaela were sharing a pot of tea. They had a lot of catching up to do.

The friends sat down at their table, which was full of the most divine-looking cakes.

"All this adventure has given me the most enormous appetite!" said Juno with a laugh as they all tucked in.

Evie's favorites were the cloudberry puffs. They were sprinkled with tiny rain crystals that exploded in her mouth!

"Well, Evie," said Skye. "I know I said that Unicorn Riding Camp would be fun, but I didn't think for a minute that it would be quite so exciting!"

"I don't think any of us will be awake for the midnight feast tonight," said Wanda. "I'm exhausted."

"Can you stay, Evie?" asked Storm.

"I'd love to," said Evie, "but we really have to get back so that I can settle all my ponies for the night."

"You must come for the next Riding Camp now that you're part of our team," said Wanda.

The friends all agreed that Evie, Diamond and, of course, Sparkles would always be welcome. Then they got up to help Evie prepare for the ride home. Professor Nimbus and Raphaela came over to say goodbye.

"Thank you for coming to our camp," said Raphaela. "You've been a great team player."

"Who knows," added Professor Nimbus, "if you keep training at Unicorn Riding Camp, you may be selected for the Olympic team one day!"

When they got to the stables, Evie could see that her unicorn was tired from the day's adventures.

"Don't worry, Diamond," said Evie. "We'll soon be home. But first we have to say goodbye to all our friends."

The unicorns whickered and touched noses, saying their unicorn goodbyes.

"We'll see you all next time!" said Evie as she mounted Diamond using the technique Raphaela had taught them. "Hope you all have fun at camp tomorrow!"

"We will!" Wanda said with a smile.

The thunderstorm was over and the sunset clouds had begun to glow with warm pinks. As soon as Diamond trotted out through the golden gate, Evie and Sparkles spotted the tunnel of trees.

When they arrived at Starlight Stables, the sun was setting behind the Golden Mountain and the clouds burned with pinks, reds, and magentas. There, waiting beside Diamond's stable door, was Diamond's kit. A riding jacket was folded neatly on top of the brushes.

"It's a unicorn rider's jacket for the Olympic team," said Evie as she tried it on.

It didn't fit her at all; it was far too big. Evie tried to hide her disappointment and Sparkles comforted her with a purr.

"Of course, Sparkles," Evie said with a smile. "This isn't for me to wear now. It's for when I'm ready for the team—when I'm older and I've perfected all the skills an Olympic rider needs."

Evie hugged her beautiful new riding jacket.

"Thank you, cloud sprites," she said, "and thank you, Diamond. What a very special unicorn!"

"Meow!" said Sparkles as he chased a tiny pink cloudlet that floated across the yard.

Pony Facts & Activities

Evie

LIVES AT:
Starlight Castle

FAVORITE FOOD:
Apple-blossom ice cream

FAVORITE PASTIME:
Going on adventures
with magic ponies

FAVORITE FLOWER:
Violets

FANTASY JOB:
Training unicorns
for the Olympics

Diamond

BREED:
Connemara pony

FEATURES:
Very strong and very good jumper

HEIGHT:
Up to fourteen hands

COLOR:
Gray is the most popular color but they can be black, bay, brown, dun, roan, and chestnut.

Step-by-Step

Evie goes to riding camp to learn how to be an even better rider. Can you put these steps to riding a pony in the right order? Once you've done this, put the other pony facts in order.

A.

Getting your horse ready to ride

Check that the saddle is on securely.
Put the bridle on.
Check that your pony is calm and has no injuries.
Mount your pony.
Put the saddle on.
Put your foot in the stirrup.
Make sure your riding hat is on securely.

B.
After a ride

Take off the saddle.
Loosen the saddle slightly.
Take off the bridle.
Walk the horse around until it is cool.
Comb where the saddle was.
Put your pony back in its stable or pasture.

C.
The speeds of a horse

Gallop
Trot
Halt
Walk
Canter

ANSWERS: A) 3, 5, 2, 1, 7, 6, 4 / B) 2, 4, 3, 1, 5, 6 / C) 3, 4, 2, 5, 1

Unicorn Facts

Unicorns have appeared in many stories throughout history. The descriptions of them have varied— some are described as ponylike, white with golden horns, while others are more goatlike! The word "unicorn" means "single horn," and all unicorns in history have had this in common. Unicorns are supposed to have great powers but are very hard to catch.

Their tears and blood are supposed to have healing powers. For this reason there have always been people trying to catch them. Unicorns are mentioned in many historical texts, but a lot of these authors could actually be confusing them with rhinoceroses, white deer, and narwhals.

Scrambles

Can you unscramble these pony words?
Check your answers at the bottom of the page.

1. aerm
2. olaf
3. adleds
4. irens
5. fhoo
6. stpareu
7. bletsa
8. phrsdujo
9. nypo
10. ital

ANSWERS: 1. MARE 2. FOAL 3. SADDLE 4. REINS 5. HOOF 6. PASTURE 7. STABLE 8. JODHPURS 9. PONY 10. TAIL

Fantasy Job

Evie had such fun at Unicorn Riding Camp that she'd love to compete in the Unicorn Olympics one day. What would be your fantasy job?

Looking for another great book?
Find it
IN THE MIDDLE.

Fun, fantastic books for kids
in the in-be**TWEEN** age.

IntheMiddleBooks.com

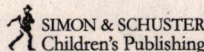 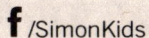 /SimonKids 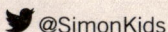 @SimonKids

READ & LEARN
with *simon* kids

Keep your child reading, learning, and having fun with Simon Kids!

A one-stop shop where you can **find downloadable resources, watch interactive author videos, browse books by reading level, and more!**

**Visit us at
SimonandSchusterPublishing.com/ReadandLearn/**

And follow us @SimonKids

 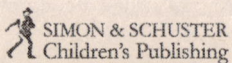 

SIMON & SCHUSTER Children's Publishing

The Forest Fairy Pony

For the magical Gwion & Arwen
—*SARAH KILBRIDE*

To Paul
—*SOPHIE TILLEY*

If you purchased this book without a cover, you should be aware that this book is stolen property. It was reported as "unsold and destroyed" to the publisher, and neither the author nor the publisher has received any payment for this "stripped book."

This book is a work of fiction. Any references to historical events, real people, or real places are used fictitiously. Other names, characters, places, and events are products of the author's imagination, and any resemblance to actual events or places or persons, living or dead, is entirely coincidental.

ALADDIN
An imprint of Simon & Schuster Children's Publishing Division
1230 Avenue of the Americas, New York, New York 10020
First Aladdin paperback edition June 2021
Text copyright © 2014 by Sarah KilBride
Cover illustration copyright © 2021 by Paula Franco
Interior illustrations based on artwork originated by Sophie Tilley copyright © 2014
Originally published in Great Britain in 2014 by Simon & Schuster UK Ltd.
Also available in an Aladdin hardcover edition.
All rights reserved, including the right of reproduction in whole or in part in any form.
ALADDIN and related logo are registered trademarks of Simon & Schuster, Inc.
For information about special discounts for bulk purchases, please contact Simon & Schuster Special Sales at 1-866-506-1949 or business@simonandschuster.com.
The Simon & Schuster Speakers Bureau can bring authors to your live event. For more information or to book an event contact the Simon & Schuster Speakers Bureau at 1-866-248-3049 or visit our website at www.simonspeakers.com.
Cover designed by Tiara Iandiorio
The text of this book was set in Sabon LT Std.
Manufactured in the United States of America 0421 OFF
2 4 6 8 10 9 7 5 3 1
Library of Congress Cataloging-in-Publication Data
Names: KilBride, Sarah, author. | Tilley, Sophie, illustrator.
Title: Forest fairy pony / by Sarah KilBride ; interior illustrations by Sophie Tilley.
Description: First Aladdin paperback edition. | New York : Aladdin, 2021. | Series: [Princess Evie ; 1] | Audience: Ages 6 to 9. | Summary: Princess Evie feels anxious about starting a new school, but she gains confidence after she visits an enchanted forest with her magical pony and helps a forest fairy named Holly welcome new forest fairy pupils on their first day of fairy school.
Identifiers: LCCN 2020051869 (print) | LCCN 2020051870 (ebook) | ISBN 9781534476288 (hardcover) | ISBN 9781534476271 (paperback) | ISBN 9781534476295 (ebook)
Subjects: CYAC: Princesses—Fiction. | Fairies—Fiction. | Schools—Fiction. | Ponies—Fiction.
Classification: LCC PZ7.K55444 Fo 2021 (print) | LCC PZ7.K55444 (ebook) | DDC [Fic]—dc23
LC record available at https://lccn.loc.gov/2020051869
LC ebook record available at https://lccn.loc.gov/2020051870

Princess EVIE

By Sarah KilBride

Interior illustrations by Sophie Tilley

The Forest Fairy Pony

ALADDIN
NEW YORK   LONDON   TORONTO   SYDNEY   NEW DELHI

CHAPTER 1
Sleepyhead

CHAPTER 2
Pony Preparations

CHAPTER 3
Old Forest Friends

CHAPTER 4
A Wonderful Welcome

CHAPTER 5
New Friends

CHAPTER 6
Pincushion in a Pickle

CHAPTER 7
A Nasty Surprise

CHAPTER 8
Campfire Catch-Up

CHAPTER 9
Forest Fairy Secrets

CHAPTER 1

Sleepyhead

Princess Evie woke with a start. *Wow, everyone must still be asleep,* thought Evie. Even Sparkles! Her kitten was usually at the door first thing in the morning waking Evie up with a noisy meow, but Starlight Castle was completely silent. Evie snuggled up under her cozy feather duvet and sighed. *I'll have to wake up earlier than this on Monday,* she thought to herself. *I'll need plenty of time to feed my ponies before getting ready for the first day at my new school!*

Evie loved her beautiful ponies. They weren't like any other ponies—each one of them was magic. There was a tunnel of trees at Starlight Stables that no one else knew about, and whenever Evie rode one of her ponies through the tunnel of trees they were whisked away on a magical adventure in a faraway land. As they galloped out of the tunnel, Evie's ponies would be magically transformed, their manes and tails glittering and their coats swirling with different colors, and Evie would be wearing an exquisite new outfit.

Evie sat up in her four-poster bed and rubbed her sleepy eyes. She smiled as she remembered all the places that her ponies had taken her and the

wonderful friends she'd met—forest fairies, cloud sprites, and even polar bears! Souvenirs from her adventures were dotted around her room: a wand from Foxwood School of Magic, a silver bracelet with the precious pink pearl from Periwinkle the mermaid, and, on the marble mantelpiece, the snowflake necklace given to her by the ice pixies. Even her purple silk pajamas were a souvenir from a magical desert sleepover with the seven star princesses!

"How am I ever going to find time to have adventures with my ponies when I'm at school?" Evie wondered out loud as she jumped down from her bed. She landed softly on her white fluffy rug and shivered. The fire had gone out in the grate and her big bedroom felt chilly. Evie quickly slipped on her coral-pink dressing gown and slippers and padded over to the window to open the thick velvet curtains. The sun was beginning to shine, making Starlight Stables sparkle.

I've got to make the most of my

magic ponies before school starts tomorrow, Evie decided. *I'm so lucky to have them.* While Evie was thinking about her ponies, she heard a loud meow at her bedroom door.

"How are you this morning, Sparkles?" asked Evie, opening the door.

Sparkles trotted in, his eyes twinkling. He looked wide-awake and ready to go!

"Meow!" said Sparkles as he began to clean his paws.

"You're right, Sparkles! It's time to get washed and dressed. We've got a busy morning ahead of us and we haven't got a second to lose. Now then," said Evie as she went to her wardrobe, "where's my pink dress and stripy tights?"

Evie pushed her wardrobe doors open to find the outfit she always wore when she went to the stables. Her wardrobe was bursting with gorgeous pink, purple, and silver clothes.

She looked at her flower dresses sewn with silk, her rainbow socks, and her fluffy boots.

"I'm going to miss wearing all these clothes," said Evie sadly. "From tomorrow on I'll have to wear a uniform."

Sparkles jumped up onto the windowsill and stepped carefully around the framed photos of Evie's ponies. He looked at Evie's uniform and then back at Evie and blinked slowly. Even though he was only a cat, Evie was sure he understood everything.

"You're right, Sparkles, my new uniform is very stylish."

It was hanging on the wardrobe's mirrored doors, ready for tomorrow.

"And of course, I'll still be able to wear all my other clothes on the weekends." This thought cheered Evie up and soon she was washed, dressed, and ready for breakfast.

Evie met Sparkles at the top of the huge staircase that spiraled down to the hall. It was lined with golden framed portraits of Evie's ancestors. Some of them were on horseback, and Evie always wondered whether they rode through the tunnel of trees like she did—the castle was full of ornaments and trinkets from faraway places.

"On your mark, get set, go!"

They raced past the paintings, through the echoing hall, and down into the kitchen.

"Sparkles—you won again!" laughed Evie. "You always do!"

The table was set with ruby raspberries, silver-birch syrup, and delicious homemade jams. Evie tucked into her breakfast, and by the time she was spreading her favorite jam onto her crumpets, Sparkles's bowl was empty and the little kitten was busy licking his paws. Sparkles loved the weekends because he always had kippers for breakfast. What a treat!

"I wish you could come to school with me. I won't know anyone." Evie tried to imagine her new classroom and teacher. She felt a little shiver and couldn't decide whether she was feeling nervous or excited.

CHAPTER 2

Pony Preparations

"Come on," said Evie as she put on her rain boots, "let's go and feed the ponies." Evie loved this part of the day—her ponies were always so glad to see her. They whinnied and neighed as soon as they heard Evie and her kitten making their way through the castle grounds. "Let's take the shortcut through the orchard," said Evie, "and we can collect some windfall apples for a tasty pony treat!"

Evie could see Silver waiting for her

at the gate with her friends Shimmer and Indigo. Silver was a pretty Welsh mountain pony and Evie's smallest, but without a doubt she was the strongest pony Evie had ever met! Star, Evie's spirited Arab, neighed from her stable. Star loved nothing more than racing along the mountaintops with the

wind in her mane. All her ponies were extremely special and Evie loved each one of them.

There was always so much to do at Starlight Stables, but the first job was to make sure her ponies were all happy and to give them fresh water. The sun was beginning to warm the autumn air, and little leaves fluttered from the trees. As Evie led her ponies from the field and tied them in the stable yard, Sparkles played with the leaves, jumping and pouncing and trying to bat them with his paws.

It wasn't long before Evie called over to her kitten, "Time to get to work, Sparkles."

It wasn't just Evie's ponies that enjoyed eating oats! Sparkles had the very important job of making sure Starlight Stables was free of rats and mice. Evie opened the door and Sparkles dashed in to inspect the feed shed.

After a few minutes, he gave a loud "all clear" meow!

"Phew!" said Evie.

Evie went in and measured out the oats. Each one of her ponies had a different amount because they were all different shapes and sizes. Some of Evie's ponies were energetic, like her Arab, Star, while others liked to take things a little easier! Added to that, some of them spent their time out in the fields, enjoying the grass, while others lived in their stables.

While the ponies were enjoying their breakfasts, Evie got her grooming kit from the tack room and brushed their coats and cleaned out their feet. She checked that her ponies didn't have any injuries and chatted away to them.

"If anyone heard me talking to you like this, Willow," said Evie as she looked over her little New Forest pony's feet, "they might think I was crazy!" But Evie knew talking to her ponies made them feel calm.

Willow stood at thirteen hands. Like all New Forests, she was gentle and very sure-footed. As Evie combed out her thick mane, Willow nudged her gently.

"You're right, Willow," said Evie. "It is the perfect day for an adventure."

Evie went to the tack room to get

her pony's saddle and bridle. The walls were lined with saddle racks and hooks for every bridle and halter.

Hanging next to Willow's saddle were all her rosettes. Although Willow wasn't the fastest pony at Starlight Stables, she was a great jumper and she loved going to cross-country events with Evie.

It didn't take long to saddle Willow up.

Evie was about to mount when she remembered something very important!

"Of course we can't go yet! We have to take my backpack of useful things!" Evie could never go through the tunnel of trees without her backpack—there was always something in it that they needed.

When Sparkles saw Evie putting the backpack on, he raced across the yard and sprang up into the saddle. He adored going on adventures with Evie and her magic ponies; they always had so much fun.

Soon Willow was trotting out of Starlight Stables, taking Evie and Sparkles toward the tunnel of trees. Evie closed her eyes and took a deep breath.

Where would it take them today?

CHAPTER 3

Old Forest Friends

"What a beautiful forest," gasped Evie as they came into a clearing of tall trees.

Willow's coat swirled with autumn colors and her mane was decorated with shining berries. Sparkling dewdrops glimmered like diamonds along her browband.

A gentle breeze blew through the trees, but Evie was nice and warm. She was wearing a scarf as delicate as a cobweb and a pale green felt jacket that tied at the waist with a ribbon the

color of blackberries. Her skirt was layered with different shades of pink silk like the petals of a wild rose.

Willow neighed as they came to a halt. "You're right, Willow, we have been here before—for the forest fairy fashion show. We helped the forest fairies to make their outfits with spiders' webs and dewdrops."

"And you helped us to solve the mystery of the stolen dresses," said a voice from above. "Welcome back."

Evie looked up.

"Holly!" laughed Evie. "How lovely to see you again!"

The forest fairy fluttered down from her branch and gave Evie a hug. She was a little bit older and taller than Evie, and her blue eyes sparkled with happiness to see her friend again.

"I'm so glad you've come back," said the forest fairy, stroking Willow's muzzle. "We've got a busy day ahead of us. Let's go to the Acorn Café and I'll tell you all about it."

Holly led the way, flying in and out of the trees. Evie felt the warm autumn sun on her face and the fresh crisp air. It wasn't long before Evie and Holly were busily catching up on each other's news.

"I've been chosen to teach all the new fairies how to become magic forest fairies," said Holly. "They'll be arriving in a little while. As it's their first day at forest fairy school, I'll help them settle in with a fun task before teaching them all about forest magic."

"I'm starting a new school too," said Evie. "I'm feeling a bit nervous about it."

"When do you start?" asked Holly.

"Tomorrow," said Evie. "I hope my

new teacher will be as kind as you, Holly, and gives us time to settle in." Holly fluttered down and held Evie's hand.

"I feel so unsure about everything. There are so many things I want to know," said Evie, trying to smile. "What will the other girls be like? What happens at break times? The more I think about it, the more fluttery I feel!"

Holly smiled at her friend. "What you're feeling is completely natural. All the new fairies will be feeling nervous today, but it won't take long for the fun to start and the friendships to begin. Just you see."

In no time at all, they arrived at the Acorn Café.

"Here we are, Willow," said Evie, giving her pony one of the windfall apples from Starlight Castle's orchard and some fresh water.

"Mmmm, let's order some hazelnut

shakes," said Holly, looking at the menu. "They're yummy!"

They sat down at a table with their delicious shakes. Holly made a list of things to do with her magic quill, which was made from a magnificent golden feather.

"We have got a busy morning ahead

of us!" said Evie, looking at the long list. "We'd better get started."

"Let's split up," said Holly, finishing her shake. "That way we'll get everything done quickly. Willow can take you into the forest to collect birch bark and firewood for the campfire. See you back in the Magic Dell!"

CHAPTER 4

A Wonderful Welcome

Evie and Sparkles hopped onto Willow and disappeared into the forest while Holly made a list of all the new fairies' names. As she called out each name, her magic quill wrote them down:

"Ivy, Arwen, Rose, Sylvette, Rowan, Bryony, Juniper, Violet, Faye . . ."

When she'd finished, Holly made a map for each fairy. As she described the woods, her magic quill drew a map of Bluebell Forest. Evie didn't need one to find the silver birch trees because her New Forest pony knew exactly where to go.

"This papery birch bark is perfect for starting campfires," said Evie as she carefully peeled the birch tree's trunk. Then Sparkles and Willow helped her find dry sticks for kindling.

Evie met Holly back at the Magic Dell and they built the campfire.

"We'll light it at the end of the day," said Holly as they arranged cushions on the forest floor.

"We've only got ten minutes before the new fairies arrive!" said Evie. "And we've still got lots to do!"

"I'll make the signposts and find a wand for each fairy," said Holly, looking at the list. "Could you decorate

these baskets please, Evie? They need to be sorted into pairs and for each pair to look identical."

Evie looked at the little baskets.

"Shall I paint each pair the same color?" she asked.

"That's a great idea, but we haven't got time for the paint to dry," said Holly. "I'm sure you'll think of something, though!"

Holly set to work drawing beautiful signs with her magic quill and then whizzed off into the forest to put the signs up, while Evie sorted the baskets into pairs.

"How am I ever going to make these pairs look identical, Sparkles?" asked Evie, picking up two of the baskets. Her kitten began diving about in the fallen leaves.

"What a brilliant idea, Sparkles! Of course—I'll decorate each pair with a different type of leaf!"

Evie set to work. She decorated two of the baskets with oak leaves and

acorns, and another two with orange beech leaves and beech nuts. Sparkles helped her collect a pile of pretty rowan leaves and red berries for the next two. Very soon all the baskets were matching pairs.

When Holly returned, she was delighted. "They look lovely," she smiled.

But Evie was looking a little confused.

"There are nine names on the register," she said. "But we've got ten baskets."

"One of them is yours," smiled Holly, popping a wand into each basket. "I hope you don't mind, but I had an odd number of fairies in my class, so I needed you to help make up a pair."

"No problem," said Evie, who was happy to help her friend.

Now they were ready for the new forest fairies!

One after another, the new fairies began to arrive at the Magic Dell. Some of them looked a little bit lost. Some of them looked a little bit sad. Some fluttered at the edges of the circle and

a few laughed a little too loud. Evie realized that they were all feeling nervous and that each of them showed their nerves in a different way.

Holly, Evie, and Sparkles tried to make the fairies feel better with a friendly smile. They asked each fairy their name and gave them each a basket. Everyone sat down on the comfy cushions and the nervous chattering stopped. The forest fell silent.

"Welcome to Bluebell Forest," smiled Holly. "Today is all about learning how to fly and find your way in this magic forest. Take your time and use all your senses to navigate.

"In a few minutes you will be exploring the forest and making your very own fairy crowns. You will have a partner to help you and I'll never be far away."

Evie looked around the circle as Holly talked and wondered which fairy was going to be her partner.

"Your partner is the fairy with the same basket as you."

Evie's basket was decorated with ivy leaves.

She looked around and soon spotted the other fairy with an ivy basket. The fairy had golden hair and a lovely smile. Evie walked over to her.

"Hello," she said. "I'm Evie."

"I'm Arwen," smiled her partner. "Is that your magic forest pony?"

"Yes, that's Willow," said Evie. "She'd love to take us into the forest. Come on!"

Evie and Sparkles hopped up onto Willow's back, while Arwen hovered above them.

"You will discover that the forest

is full of life; it's home to many creatures. Work with them and they will help your magic," said Holly. "Everyone needs to be back here with their finished crowns by the time the blackbirds begin to sing."

The fairies started looking at their maps and getting ready to leave. Soon they were all fluttering into Bluebell Forest with their partners.

CHAPTER 5

New Friends

"I've never flown in the forest before," said Arwen nervously as she took off. "I'm not sure if I'm good enough to do it."

"Don't worry," said Evie, "we'll take it slow. I think it's a bit like riding a pony through the forest—keep your balance and don't rush. Once you get the hang of it, you'll love it—we do, don't we, Willow?"

Willow tossed her mane and flicked her lovely tail.

"The secret is to look where you're going but remember to keep your eyes open for any challenges up ahead. You don't want a nasty surprise like a branch in the face!"

Willow walked in and out of the trees. Arwen flew above the New Forest pony and began to feel more confident.

"You're looking great!" said Evie. "Are you ready to go a bit faster?"

"Absolutely!" The little fairy smiled.

Willow began to trot along the forest path.

"When you're coming to a corner, make sure you're not going too fast. You don't want to lose your balance!" said Evie. Arwen watched how Evie helped to steer Willow and slow her down if there was a tight corner coming up. Arwen copied this and soon she was weaving through the trees effortlessly.

"This is brilliant!" laughed Arwen

as they sailed over ditches. "You and Willow are such a great team!"

Arwen was right—Willow loved riding cross-country with Evie, and Evie was a careful rider. She could feel the fresh air whiz past them as they raced through the forest. They were having so much fun racing up slopes and following streams that for a while they forgot their task!

It was only when Willow came to a halt by a cluster of hazel trees draped with strings of little leaves and red berries that the friends remembered they had to make forest fairy crowns.

"Why don't we use these?" said Evie. "We can twist the stems to make a crown."

Arwen and Evie each took a string of leaves and twisted it into a circle.

"Let's try them on," said Arwen.

"They'll look really beautiful when we decorate them," said Evie, helping Arwen to tighten her crown a little.

"You're right, but what can we use?"

At that moment a beautiful gold feather floated down from the tree. Shimmering on a branch above was the most striking golden bird.

"Please, could we have a few more of your feathers?" asked Evie hopefully, carefully fixing the feather onto Arwen's crown.

The bird looked down at them, her

bright eyes flickering like flames.

"I think she's a phoenix," whispered Evie. "I've read about them in one of the old books in Starlight Castle's library. I thought they were mythical creatures."

The golden bird screeched at them, making poor Willow jump and Sparkles shake. It was a shock that such a beautiful bird could make such a terrible sound!

"She sounds real to me!" said Arwen. The phoenix squawked again.

"I think she's trying to tell us something," said Evie, putting her hands over her ears. "Perhaps you could try some forest magic to translate."

"I've never tried any forest magic

before," said Arwen, carefully taking her wand out of her basket. "But I'll give it a try."

"Take your time," said Evie.

Arwen closed her eyes and after a few seconds began whispering some magic forest words:

*"Blow, wind, blow,
Golden bird, do not shriek.
Flow, words, flow,
Golden words from your beak.
Leaves shiver, leaves fall,
Forest creature, tell me all."*

Tiny green sparks fizzed and whizzed from the tip of the wand and floated above their heads.

The phoenix stood tall and opened her mouth, but instead of letting out another shrill shriek, she said in a proud voice:

*"Look around the forest trees,
Listen to the forest breeze.
A little pincushion trying to sleep,
Help him—he's in trouble deep.
When you've finished this task at hand,
I will help you gild your band."*

And with that, she flew a little farther up into the tree.

"I hope you're better at solving riddles than I am," said Evie.

"Hmm," said Arwen thoughtfully. "I think the second part of the riddle means the phoenix will help us with our crowns if we help someone in the forest. But I don't know who they are or where we'll find them."

Arwen and Evie looked at the map of Bluebell Forest, searching for clues.

"A pincushion would be used by someone sewing," said Evie. "Perhaps they're making outfits with spiderweb thread like we did for the fashion show."

"But where would they be?" asked Arwen. Willow neighed loudly.

"I think Willow knows," said Evie.

CHAPTER 6

Pincushion in a Pickle

In just a few moments, Evie and Sparkles were cantering through the forest on Willow's back, with Arwen flying above. As they went deeper into the forest, Willow had to jump branches and trees that had fallen across the path.

"I love the way you help Willow jump, Evie," Arwen called down. Evie leaned forward as Willow took off over a branch.

"If there's something in the way, you have to make sure you're going at it straight and steady. It's the same for you, Arwen, when you're flying over obstacles."

"I think Willow trusts you because you never push her too hard."

"I trust her too," smiled Evie. "We look out for each other."

It was true Willow trusted Evie; the brave little pony didn't mind if she couldn't see where she was going to land after taking off over a fallen branch because she knew Evie would never ask too much of her.

Arwen flew above them, the wind whistling through her hair.

"Hold on to your crown, Evie," she called down to her friend as they raced through the trees.

After a short while, they came to a

clearing with a tall sycamore tree. Evie stroked Willow's neck.

"Good girl," she smiled as she and Sparkles hopped down from the saddle.

"Now all we need to find is a pincushion," said Arwen, landing gently and looking through the piles of autumn leaves.

But the friends couldn't find anything like a pincushion.

"Maybe we're not in the right place after all," said Evie.

They began to walk through the shady forest, searching the mossy floor, when Sparkles's whiskers began to twitch.

"Whatever's the matter, Sparkles?" said Evie.

Willow stopped and the little kitten jumped about and started searching around in the roots of a tree.

Evie spotted a shiny nose and a pair of bright eyes peeping at them from the shadows—and out popped a baby hedgehog!

"A little pincushion!" she cried. "Sparkles, you've solved the riddle!"

The little hedgehog came out of his hiding place and began making excitable squeaky noises.

"How are we going to help this little hedgehog out?" said Arwen.

"What on earth is he trying to tell us?" asked Evie.

Arwen whisked out her wand and performed the translation spell:

"Blow, wind, blow,
Prickly hedgehog, do not squeak.
Flow, words, flow,
Little hedge pig, try to speak.
Leaves shiver, leaves fall,
Forest creature, tell me all."

Tiny green sparks fizzed and whizzed again from the tip of her wand and floated above them.

"Follow me. Come along—I want to show you something. I've been working hard all day. Come and have a little look; come and see what I've built. It's beautiful, my new house. I've tried to wake up my friends to show them, but they're all asleep. They usually wake up around now to look for some nice berries to eat. Come on, keep up . . ." The little hedgehog's words tumbled out.

"What a chatterbox!" giggled Evie.

They had quite a job keeping up with the little creature, who was chittering away as he led them along the forest path. He was surprisingly fast and it seemed that he was in quite a hurry.

"I never knew hedgehogs could move so quickly," said Arwen.

He brought them to a pile of very untidy sticks and leaves.

"Here it is!" he said proudly. "My new home."

Arwen and Evie looked at each other, not sure what to say.

Evie peeped inside and could see a muddy puddle.

"It's not very cozy," she said.

"It's my first hibernation and I've worked very hard collecting all these

leaves and sticks. It's taken me a long, long, long time to build this."

Evie didn't want to hurt the little hedgehog's feelings.

"How very clever of you to disguise your house to look like a pile of old leaves," she smiled. "But when the winter comes and it gets colder, I'm sure you'd like it to be nice and dry inside."

"Perhaps we could build your nest somewhere else, somewhere drier," said Arwen. "I think Sparkles may have found just the spot!"

Sparkles was sitting in a sheltered patch beneath a little bush, next to some brambles.

"Perfect," said the hedgehog. "I love blackberries!"

"You won't have to go far for lunch!" agreed Arwen.

The friends set to work, helping the little hedgehog to build his winter nest.

"We'll need lots of dry leaves, little sticks, grass, and some moss," said Evie.

"These might do," said Arwen with an armful of leaves.

Suddenly the girls heard the sound of a rotten branch snapping. They froze. It felt like someone was watching them—but who could it be?

Arwen took hold of her wand and searched the undergrowth. The air

began to shimmer and, after a moment, Holly appeared!

"I didn't know you could make yourself invisible!" laughed Evie, relieved to see it was her friend.

"I've come to see how you're doing," said Holly.

"We've started our crowns," said Arwen. Evie and Arwen showed Holly their handiwork. "But we need to help this little pincushion before we can finish them."

"I'm so pleased you're helping a forest creature," said Holly. "Keep up the good work! I can't wait to see your beautiful crowns when they're finished." And with that, Holly gave them both a quick hug and was gone!

Arwen and Evie helped the hedgehog make a pile with the leaves, moss, and

grass they had collected. The little hedgehog then climbed to the top of the mound and burrowed inside, turning around and around, packing the leaves flat.

Together, they had made a beautiful cozy nest with thick walls.

"Let's celebrate with a feast!" said the delighted hedgehog, and they all helped themselves to the delicious blackberries growing on the bramble next door.

The berries were very juicy and soon Evie, Arwen, and the little hedgehog

were covered in the berries' purple juices.

"I'll see if I've got anything to wipe our fingers with," said Evie as she opened up her backpack of useful things. She pulled out a pink silk handkerchief and, as she did so, a single woolen mitten fell out too.

"I don't think that'll be any good at cleaning us up," laughed Arwen, "but it might help a little hedgehog keep snug in the winter."

Arwen was right! It made a perfect bed for the hedgehog. Evie carefully laid it in his nest.

"Do you know the quickest way back to the phoenix?" asked Evie. But the little hedgehog didn't hear her, as he was already scurrying away to wake up his friends and invite them to his nest-warming party!

"We'll find our way back," said Arwen. "I feel like I'm getting to know the forest."

"It won't take us long," said Evie. "Especially with Willow to carry us!"

CHAPTER 7

A Nasty Surprise

They set off along the forest path. It was just as well that Willow was sure-footed because the ground soon changed from being soft and squidgy to stony and slippery. One minute Willow was trotting through piles of crisp leaves that reached her feathery fetlocks and the next she was picking her way through sticky mud.

Arwen was relieved she could fly over this rough terrain, and Sparkles was very glad that he didn't have to walk through it, especially the mud!

When they came to some fallen branches, Willow refused to jump even a small one. Evie knew something was not right.

"What's wrong, Willow?" whispered Evie as she turned Willow to take the jump again, and then Evie realized.

"You're limping," she cried. Evie dismounted right away. When she looked into Willow's eyes, she could see her pony was in pain.

"What if it's something serious?" Evie's heart was pounding, but she had to control her feeling of panic.

"It's her front right leg," said Arwen. The little fairy held Willow's reins and talked quietly to her to reassure her and keep her calm.

"I can't see any cuts or scratches," said Evie, peering closely at her pony's leg.

Gently, she ran her hand over Willow's shoulder and leg to check for swelling or heat. Willow didn't flinch. Next Evie carefully picked up her pony's hoof.

"No wonder you're limping, Willow," gasped Evie. "You've got a sharp stone lodged in your hoof."

It was near the heart-shaped pad at the center of the hoof, called the frog. Luckily, Evie kept her hoof pick in her backpack, but she knew she would have to be extra careful as Willow's hoof would be more sensitive than usual.

"You're going to have to be a very brave pony," she said as she cautiously removed the forest debris around the stone. "Let's hope it hasn't damaged your hoof."

They were lucky—the stone fell out from Willow's hoof and Evie saw that, although her sole wasn't punctured, there was a nasty purple bruise. Evie knew that this would be very painful for quite some time.

"The best treatment is to rest for a few days," said Evie.

"But you can't stay here in the

middle of the forest," said Arwen.

A golden feather floated down. There above the girls was the shimmering phoenix.

"Can you help us, phoenix?" asked Evie.

The golden bird flew down and landed on Arwen's shoulder.

"Together we can heal Willow," the phoenix said. "Follow me, Arwen."

And with that, they disappeared into the forest. Evie turned to her pony and blinked back tears.

She knew she had to be brave for Willow's sake, but she could see her pony was in a lot of pain and Evie began to wonder if it was her fault. As Evie stroked Willow, she could feel her pony relax and lean in to her.

"We'll look after you," she whispered in her ear. "Just you see."

After a few minutes Arwen returned with a handful of magic herbs. The phoenix wasn't far behind Arwen, with some moss in her beak.

"These will heal Willow's hoof," said Arwen.

She mixed the herbs, moss, and some clay from the ground and made a poultice. She placed the dressing gently onto Willow's bruise. Then the phoenix rested her magical golden wings on the injured hoof and, as she did this, Arwen lifted her wand and tiny green sparks floated from the tip. Willow closed her eyes as the magic began to glow, and Arwen and the phoenix worked together to heal Willow's hoof.

"I think that's done the trick," said Arwen as she gently took the poultice away. "Yes, your bruise has vanished."

"Thank you," smiled Evie. Tears welled up in her eyes again, but this time they were tears of happiness! She was so relieved to see that her pony's injury was healed. Willow tossed her long mane and stamped her foot as if she were raring to go!

"Before you leave," said the phoenix, "look closely at this tree."

"It's hollow!" said Evie.

"It's a fairy tree," explained the golden bird.

Arwen took a peek inside the hollow trunk.

"It's full of treasure!" she gasped.

Inside was a pile of little sycamore leaves made from real gold, and glittering among them were jewels that looked just like shining blackberries.

"Our crowns will be magnificent," said Evie. "Thank you, phoenix."

The phoenix bowed her head majestically, and with that, she disappeared into the golden canopy of the forest.

"Let me help you, Evie," said Arwen.

The girls threaded the precious leaves and berries into their forest crowns and even laced a few into Willow's mane. When they had finished, there were still some golden leaves and jewels left.

"Let's take these back for the others," Evie suggested.

"Good idea, Evie!"

Willow's hoof was so much better that she was able to trot along the forest path, taking Evie and Sparkles back to the dell. Arwen fluttered along after them, carefully carrying her basket of treasure.

As they got closer to the Magic Dell, they could see wisps of smoke and the air was full of blackbirds' song and fairies' laughter. It sounded like everyone had enjoyed their first day.

CHAPTER 8

Campfire Catch-Up

"Welcome back!" smiled Holly. "I hope you've had fun in the forest—I can't wait to hear about it!"

Soon all the fairies had returned safely back to the dell and were sitting around the campfire, warm and happy.

"I'm so glad you enjoyed your forest adventures," said Holly. "Now, who wants to go first and tell everyone about their day?"

Faye put up her hand and she and her partner began to tell everyone how they had helped a little squirrel hide all the hazelnuts he'd collected for his winter store. As they told their story, they handed out some of the deliciously crunchy nuts.

Next the fairies listened to how Bryony and Violet had made warm winter coats for a family of dormice. They had used fur from the insides of chestnut shells and had brought a basketful of the creamy chestnuts to roast in the glowing fire.

Then it was Evie and Arwen's turn to tell their story of how they had helped the little hedgehog build his nest. Everyone was looking forward to the blackberries Arwen and Evie had picked with the hedgehog, and a few fairies looked a bit disappointed when Evie told them they had eaten them all.

"We've got something else to share with you," said Arwen.

Evie and Arwen handed out the gold leaves and bright jewels that

they had found in the fairy tree. The fairies gasped and wove them into their crowns, where they sparkled and glittered in the firelight. As the

fairies took turns telling their stories, it became obvious that they had all helped forest creatures in some way, and in return the magnificent golden phoenix had helped each of them.

Everyone had enjoyed their first day, even though they had all felt nervous about it at the start. It was clear that friendships had already begun to blossom and everyone was looking forward to their second day in the forest.

"We worry about meeting new people and going to new places," said Holly. "It's impossible to imagine what it's going to be like, and that can make us feel anxious, but new people and new places can be fun too. First days are the start of an adventure!"

Soon the campfire was smoldering and it was time to go home. The fairies said goodbye to Sparkles, Willow, and Evie and wished Evie luck for her first day.

"Try not to worry about tomorrow," smiled little Faye.

"Everyone will be feeling the same as you," said Sylvette.

Bryony gave Evie a hug. "Stay calm and smile."

"And remember that the people

around you won't be strangers for long—soon they will be your friends," said Ivy and Violet, holding hands.

"Soon you'll know everyone's names and share many lovely times with your newfound friends," smiled Rowan and Rose, looking tired but happy. All the fairies fluttered up into the air and followed Juniper through the trees.

"Thank you for helping make my first day such an adventure," said Arwen, giving her new friend a hug.

"Thank you for looking after Willow," said Evie. "We've certainly had an unforgettable time!"

"Good luck tomorrow, and remember, it's the beginning of a great adventure," said Arwen.

"Thank you for all your help today, Evie. I hope you enjoy your first day

at school," said Holly, and then she whispered a forest fairy secret into Evie's ear.

Willow neighed as she took Evie and Sparkles along the forest path back to the tunnel of trees.

CHAPTER 9

Forest Fairy Secrets

Evie got back to Starlight Stables and untacked Willow and groomed her coat. When she cleaned out her hooves, it was hard to believe that Willow had been injured that day—there wasn't a mark to be seen.

"Thank you for taking me back to the forest, Willow. I've had a magical day. It was great to catch up with my old friend Holly and to make some lovely new friends too!"

Evie knew she should have an early night, but before she and Sparkles

could go back to the castle for some supper and to get some sleep, she had to clean her ponies' stables and make sure they were ready for the night. Evie checked their water and gave them all fresh hay. She fed Willow some tasty carrots from the vegetable garden.

"I think you deserve a treat for working so hard and for being so brave today," she smiled, giving her pony a gentle hug.

When Evie was in her room, she emptied her backpack out onto her desk. She was looking for some nice pens and pencils to put in her new pencil case for tomorrow, when out fell a magnificent golden feather. She looked at the feather closely and realized what it was.

"It's a magic quill like Holly's," Evie gasped. "What a fantastic present. I'm sure it'll come in handy, especially when I have to do my homework. Thank you, forest fairies."

Sparkles watched Evie pack her

schoolbag and check her uniform.

"Do you know, Sparkles, I think I'm looking forward to tomorrow! I can't wait to make some new friends!"

Sparkles began purring loudly, then curled himself up into a little ball on Evie's comfy bed. He was exhausted!

"I'd better have an early night as well! There's nothing worse than being too tired to enjoy an adventure."

That night, Evie lay in her soft

feather bed and listened to the storm that was blowing around Starlight Castle's towers. She thought about her ponies, safe in their stables, and the animals they'd met in the forest—the little hedgehog snug in his nest and the proud phoenix in his golden tree. Evie smiled and huddled up under her toasty duvet; she knew she was going to sleep well.

The next morning Evie woke to the

sound of her alarm clock. She'd set it extra early so she would have time to get ready for her first day without having to race around.

She hopped down from her bed and opened the curtains. The sky was clear and the sun was beginning to rise.

"Good morning, Starlight Stables," she smiled. "Today I'm going to have another adventure—my first day at my new school!"

When Evie had finished putting on her uniform, she turned to Sparkles, who was sitting on the windowsill.

"What do you think, Sparkles?"

Her little kitten looked carefully at Evie's pretty school shoes with their silver buckles and began to purr. After breakfast the two of them trotted down to the stables. Evie fed her ponies their breakfast.

"I'll tell you all about my first day when I get back," she whispered to Willow. Willow whinnied as if to wish Evie luck.

It was time to go. As Evie shut the gate, she felt a little flutter of nervousness, or was it excitement? The wind blew and leaves flew around her. Evie remembered Holly's forest fairy secret and she held out her hand and caught a golden leaf.

With the leaf held in both hands, Evie closed her eyes, just as Holly had told her to do, then blew the leaf back into the wind, and made her wish:

"I wish that . . .

. . . everyone has a magical first day."

Pony Facts
&
Activities

Evie

LIVES AT:
Starlight Castle

FAVORITE COLOR:
Purple

FAVORITE FRUIT:
Wild strawberries

FAVORITE FLOWER:
Violets

FANTASY JOB:
Training unicorns for the Olympics

Willow

BREED:
New Forest Pony

FEATURES:
Small size
Neat, pointed ears
Big, bold eyes
Wide forehead

HEIGHT:
From twelve hands to fourteen hands

COLOR:
Normally bay, brown, or gray but can be chestnut, roan, or black. They can have some white markings on their heads or legs.

Pony Colors

Bay
These ponies have a brown body
and black points.

Black
It's very rare to see a completely black
pony, as to be classed as black they
must not have brown hair.

Brown
A brown pony is dark brown all over
and has brown points.

Chestnut
These are reddish brown and do not have any black on them.

Dun
These are pale brown, with black legs and a dark stripe along their backs.

Gray
Gray ponies are often described as white as they can be so light in color.

Palomino
These pretty ponies are gold colored with white manes or tails.

Piebald
A black pony with white patches.

Roan
A bay, black, or chestnut pony that has white hairs sprinkled through its coat.

Skewbald
Any color pony, apart from black, that has white patches.

True or False?

Here are some facts about Evie and her ponies. Decide which are true and which are false, then check your answers at the bottom of the page.

Willow is a Connemara pony.

Willow is twelve hands tall.

Evie has never met Holly before.

The Forest Fairies can't fly.

Hedgehogs hibernate.

The phoenix is a bright blue bird.

Holly gives Evie a magic golden quill.

ANSWERS: 1F 2T 3F 4F 5T 6F 7T

Phoenix Facts

Phoenixes are mythical creatures who were famous for having long lives. Some people believed they could even live for more than five hundred years! The myth goes that, when the time came for their end of their lives, they built a nest and then burst into flames. From their ashes, a new phoenix would arise. Their links with fire and flames were even stronger due to their red-and-golden-colored feathers. This led to them sometimes being called

"firebirds." They were extremely wise and kind creatures who always helped those in need. They could even heal injuries, like Willow's sore hoof, with their magic tears.

In this story, Evie could hardly believe she was lucky enough to meet this magical creature and was very grateful for her help.

Word Search

How many words from this story can you find? They can read forward, backward, diagonally, horizontally, or vertically.

T	W	S	Y	L	L	O	H	W	N
G	O	H	E	G	D	E	H	O	E
P	L	S	E	L	Y	E	I	Y	L
H	L	V	T	R	K	H	E	N	D
O	I	L	I	A	S	R	E	O	I
E	W	A	I	U	B	W	A	P	R
N	F	T	C	U	R	L	T	P	B
I	O	N	B	A	Q	H	E	R	S
X	I	P	R	I	N	C	E	S	S
P	E	L	D	D	A	S	N	W	U

FAIRY HEDGEHOG BRIDLE PONY STABLES HOLLY WILLOW PRINCESS

READ & LEARN
with *simon kids*

Keep your child reading, learning, and having fun with Simon Kids!

A one-stop shop where you can **find downloadable resources, watch interactive author videos, browse books by reading level, and more!**

Visit us at
SimonandSchusterPublishing.com/ReadandLearn/

And follow us @SimonKids

 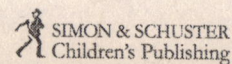